Anderson's War

Drifter Hank Anderson planned to go straight when he pinned on the town marshal's badge and tried to tame the wild and rambunctious cattle capital of Abilene. But dark secrets about his outlaw past and shady part in a Civil War massacre are being winkled out of him by the town reporter, Jane Cox.

To make matters worse, fanatical Kansan 'redlegs' are on his trail vowing revenge. And when a young lad, Newt, turns up claiming to be his son it adds to his troubles. Six guns roar as the action accelerates and fast-shooting killers rob the town bank. With Newt alongside, Hank heads after them into Indian Territory.

But even if he can recover the stolen cash he has a dilemma. Should he return with it to Jane in Abilene, or ride on to a new life in California?

Anderson's War

Jackson Davis

A Black Horse Western

ROBERT HALE · LONDON

ISBN 978-0-7090-8722-9

Robert Hale Limited
Clerkenwell House
Clerkenwell Green
London EC1R 0HT

www.halebooks.com

Typeset by
Derek Doyle & Associates, Shaw Heath
Printed and bound in Great Britain by
CPI Antony Rowe, Chippenham, Wiltshire

ONE

The lone rider was heading north across the plains at an easy lope on his grey mare. A man in his early twenties, he wore a brown corduroy coat buttoned high to the bandanna about his throat for protection against the incessant prairie wind. A low-crowned hat was pulled over his brow as his grey eyes probed the rolling grasslands. His be-jeaned legs straddled a silver-mounted Mexican saddle, his spurred boots lightly poised in the bentwood stirrups. He and the horse had covered a great distance in the past weeks, out of New Mexico, traversing the Staked Plains of northern Texas where the Comanche still prowled, crossing the Red River into Indian Territory, through a wilderness of forests, streams and mountains until he hit the well-rutted Chisholm trail.

'It ain't far now, hoss,' he muttered. 'Ye'll be gittin' your oats and I'll be sittin' on a real chair an' table taking breakfast. Almost forget what that's like.'

Hank Anderson was hungry and his stomach rumbled at the prospect. He was in a hurry to put all that bitterness and trouble of the past behind him, to start a new life in Kansas. Sure enough, as if to trumpet his arrival, he suddenly heard the wail of a locomotive's steam siren, saw a trail of smoke on the horizon and, as if by magic, a bunch of wooden houses appeared out of the early morning mist.

So it was true. There *was* a railroad and a newsprung town. A sizeable one, too. The newplaned board buildings were dominated by tall, two and three-storey saloons and hotels and a church steeple. An array of stockyards extended alongside the railroad.

Some sort of dance hall was the first place he approached on the rutted trail. A sign depicted the front view of a naked lady proclaiming to arriving drovers First Chance. As he clipped past, Anderson glanced back at the sign creaking from a pole in the wind and saw it showed the nude's backside to inform those departing Last Chance.

Next came a ramshackle assortment of huts and beer parlours, mostly shuttered this time of year, and a double line of shady-looking cribs. In the alley between, a few items of women's underwear fluttered forlornly from washing-lines.

Fifty yards further on was a more imposing two-storey saloon. Rosy Joe's was scrawled over the door. A pair of half-dressed girls hung from an open upstairs window calling, with cheeky smiles, 'Hiya, cowboy. Aincha comin' in?'

Anderson gave them a twisted grin as he rode on by. 'Not today, gals.'

But mostly, at this early dawn hour, the area was deserted, as was the town. He paused to stare at the big Iron Horse which stood hissing and shuddering, smoke trickling from its high stack. It was a long time since he had seen one. He turned the grey along past the string of boxcars and carriages, and followed the single track going along through the town's wide main street, past brand-new stores, offices, hotels and houses crowded together on both sides. There were a few early birds around and shopkeepers sweeping their sidewalks who stopped to stare at him.

'This looks like it's open,' Anderson drawled to the mare, as he reined in outside a joint named The Longhorn, stepping down into the mud, loosening the mare's cinch and letting her lap at a watertrough before hitching her to the rail. 'I'm gonna fill my belly then I'll see to you,' he said, sniffing at the appetizing scent of coffee and bacon drifting from the saloon.

His spurs jingled as he pushed through the batwing doors and ambled inside. 'Would I be right in surmising that this is Abilene?'

'That's us, mister,' a youth behind the bar yelled. 'The wickedest city in the West.'

'Good. Didn't see no sign. But seems like I've got where I aimed to go.'

A couple of business-types were standing taking their morning snifter. One was bearded, the other clean-shaven, attired in sombre black suits, and they turned to give the the dusty visitor the once over.

'What's it to be, stranger?' the fresh-faced barkeep asked.

'Gimme a whiskey with coffee, fifty-fifty,' Anderson replied, brushing the dust of travel from his jacket. He removed his worn gloves and tossed his Stetson on to a hatpeg revealing an unruly mane of brown hair. 'Ham an' eggs sunny side up.'

'Where you come from, mister?'

'Lincoln, New Mexico territory.'

'Hell, that's some ride. What brings you this way?'

'Read about you in the journals. Abilene: cowboy capital of the world. The new boom town. So, where is everybody?'

'Season ain't started yet.' The barkeep grinned. 'We're taking a well-earned rest.'

'You can say that again,' the bearded businessman butted in. 'We had a hundred and fifty thousand cattle pass through the town last summer. You couldn't move for folks out in the street.'

'So, what kinda line *you* in?' the other fellow queried.

'Fancy free.' Anderson gave a rueful smile. What had been his line was not something he was particularly proud to admit. Nor would they be pleased to hear about his past. He took the mug of steaming coffee doctored with liquor and headed for a table in the corner. 'Jest travellin',' he called over his shoulder.

Yes, it certainly did feel strange to stretch his long legs out under a table after weeks spent hunkered down over his camp-fire and sleeping under the stars. Maybe here he could start afresh, with a clean sheet, make something of his life. The 'keep brought him a wooden platter piled with ham, eggs, canned tomatoes and pinto beans and he eagerly began to shovel it down with a glow of satisfaction.

Suddenly the peace was shattered by the sound of gunshots from the street outstde. 'What 'n hell's that?' he asked.

The young barkeep went to poke his head out. 'Aw, no, it's that lunatic who was shooting up the town last night. He musta been drinkin' in Rosy Joe's and decided to give us another treat.'

'Where is he?'

They heard the crash of breaking glass. 'He's helping hisself to Sammy Samuel's jewellery. Stuffing it in his coat pockets,' the boy sang out. 'Now he's wandering up the street. Looks like he's still three sheets to the wind.'

There was the sound of more gunshots.

'He's gone into the saddler's shop.'

'Why don't somebody call the sheriff?' Anderson grunted, as he ate.

'We don't have one,' the bearded man said. 'None of 'em lasts very long.'

'Jeez,' Anderson grumbled, getting to his feet. 'Guess I'd better go put my hoss round the back for safety. Don't want her gettin' shot.'

Outside there was no sign of the miscreant, so he tethered the mare out of danger from stray bullets, jerked his Creedmore rifle from its scabbard and returned to the main street.

Suddenly, there was a shrill female scream and he saw a heavily built man, dark and sullen in a black frockcoat, come from the saddler's dragging a girl of about fifteen with him. He had a revolver swinging in one fist, his other gripped in the girl's fair hair as he hauled her across the dusty street towards the open doors of a barn. Bedroom windows had rattled open and women were looking out. A couple of men had emerged from their stores, but, as the drunk fired wildly at them, they dodged back in again.

'Oh, my God!' the 'keep wailed. 'It's young Lizzie, the saddler's daughter. I do believe he's gonna have his way with her.'

'Ain't nobody gonna do nuthin'?' Anderson asked, as the girl screamed, begged and struggled, but was dragged relentlessly away.

'What *can* we do?' the 'keep said. 'He calls himself Bloody Bob Brown. He's been bragging he's already killed six men.'

'Aw, hell,' Anderson whispered, raising his Creedmore to his shoulder. 'Why do I have to get involved?'

It was a difficult shot. They were almost a hundred yards away, and he was worried about hitting the girl. But she was down on her knees and Brown had his arm out-stretched in her hair. So he fired. Brown spun around, clutching at his left arm, dropping the girl, peering, as if amazed, along the main drag at his assailant. He raised his revolver and returned fire, backing away towards the barn.

Anderson levered a slug into the rifle's breech, but a bullet whining past his ear put him off his aim and his next slug spurted dust about Brown's boots, making him move faster.

They watched the girl scramble up, sobbing. She rushed to the arms of her father, who dragged her back into the shop for safety. Brown had taken cover in the barn.

The barkeep prompted, 'You going after him?'

'My breakfast's gittin' cold.' Anderson headed back into The Longhorn. 'He can come after me if he wants to.'

The two businessmen hurriedly took cover on the far side of the bar and debated the situation in low voices, obviously scared out of their wits. 'Bloody Bob ain't gonna give up,' the 'keep called. 'I'm sorry, mister. I can't help you.'

'What's the matter with everybody in this town?' Anderson growled, as he cut up the ham and sat with his back to the wall, forking it up with his left hand, munching the food as if unconcerned. But he edgily kept his eye on the door and didn't have to wait long. There was the ominous thump of heavy boots outside on the sidewalk.

'Where's that bastard who took a shot at me?' Bloody Bob, as he liked to be called, had hair like a wild black mop about his staring eyes, a pinched nose and thin lips amid a straggling beard. Beneath his topcoat he wore a filthy vest and torn trousers. 'I'm going to kill him.'

The eyes of the three frightened men behind the bar swivelled towards Anderson as they ducked down.

'You looking for me, half wit?' Anderson paused with his fork raised to his mouth. 'If there's one thing I can't abide it's having my breakfast disturbed by

11

some loud mouth. So, if you'll take my advice, you'll git on your hoss, git outa this town and let us have a li'l peace and quiet. OK?'

'No, it ain't OK.' Brown appeared to notice that the rifle was propped out of reach against a wall.

He grinned blackened teeth. 'Look what you done.' He pointed his revolver at the torn sleeve of his left arm which was damp with blood. 'You gotta pay.'

He turned his pistol upon the seated man. But before he could fire Anderson came up with his Remington New Army Model six-gun in his right hand, which gun he had had resting on his lap. The gun barked and Brown screamed. He went hurtling back to clatter on the floor. As blood pumped from his shirt-front he stared with agonized eyes and croaked, 'What did yer do that fer?'

'Huh?' Anderson grinned sardonically at him. 'What you think I did it for? You were trying to kill me, you buffoon.'

'Good shooting!' the bearded man shouted. 'Clean as a whistle through his chest.'

Anderson gave a hiss of relief that it was over. Gunplay always made him tense. He placed the Remington on the table. 'That ain't done my digestion no good. Now my coffee's gone cold.'

'You can have all the coffee you want, mister,' the 'keep whooped, as folks, suddenly regaining their courage, ran across and edged into the saloon. 'We got him. We shot Bloody Bob.'

Brown wasn't listening any more. He sprawled lifeless in a widening pool of his own blood. Anderson had seen too much killing in the past eight years to let it bother him much. He took a sup of the fresh coffee the 'keep poured. 'That hits the spot.'

'Sure, like you did, suh,' the 'keep replied.

A bald, rotund man, suspenders hanging around his hips and shaving soap still on his cheeks, ran in. He was Clarence Hooson, the town mayor and bank manager. 'Good Lord, Jim! Did *you* shoot him?'

'No.' The 'keep nodded towards Anderson. 'The stranger yonder.'

Upstone, the saddler, shoved through the throng, pointing at the corpse. 'That foul-mouthed ruffian would've raped my dear daughter. The abuse he gave me and my wife – it was shocking. I tried to stop him but he pulled a gun on me. I'm in your debt, stranger.'

Anderson shrugged. He finished his meal, pushing his plate away, then picked up his revolver from the table and spun the cylinder. He took a cardboard box of Hazard's .44 calibre cartridges from his coat pocket and replaced the used one. 'Thank Eli Remington. This is the hardest and surest shooting iron ever made. Solid frame over the top of the cylinder gives it added strength an' a continuous sighting groove.' He grinned again, ruefully. 'Sound like a salesman, don't I?'

The jeweller, Sammy Samuels, was demanding his property back, down on his knees, going through Bloody Bob's pockets. 'This thug got everything he deserved.'

'No virtuous woman was safe,' a woman screeched, 'with a man like him around. Poor Lizzie. I thought for a minute—' She paused, not mentioning the unmentionable. 'Thank God there's one gentleman in this town with some guts.'

'Rabid dogs gotta be put down,' the mayor said. 'Don't you worry about any repercussions, sir. I'll direct the coroner to bring in a verdict of justifiable homicide.'

'That'll make a change,' Anderson muttered, more to himself, as he stuffed the Remington into his belt holster.

'You know,' the mayor said, joining him, 'we could do with a man like you in this town. How would you like to be city marshal?'

Anderson gave a scoffing laugh. 'That would be the day.'

'I'm serious. Fifty dollars a month,' the mayor said. 'There's perks, too, plus rewards, and I hear Rosy Joe can be mighty grateful if you leave him alone. He pulls in a hundred dollars a night in the season.'

'Maybe I should go into partnership with *him*?'

'You'd have nothing but trouble. I'm making you a good offer. The town committee'll back me. We need a marshal.'

'How long did the last one live?' Anderson got to his feet, dug in his pocket. 'How much they charge for whiskey breakfast?'

Hooson raised his hands. 'Be my guest. Anything else you need, just say.'

'I pay my own way,' Anderson said, slapping down fifty cents. 'That should cover it. You got a livery, a rooming-house in this town?'

'Just along the way. Tell 'em I sent you.' As Anderson ambled to the door, the mayor called out, 'What about my offer?'

Anderson jammed his hat over his eyes, held his Creedmore over one shoulder, and muttered, 'I'll think it over.'

TWO

For the rest of that fine day Anderson ambled about town, taking a look at the jailhouse and, facing it, the Bull's Head saloon, its false front painted with an enormous red bull, just one of a dozen saloons and beer parlours in the main part of town. However all were crude compared to The Alamo.

'Whoo!' Anderson gave a low whistle of awe as he stepped through its glass doors and surveyed the paintings of Renaissance-type nudes on the walls. The main bar room was arranged with green-baize tables, keno, blackjack and roulette, mostly idle now. A polished mahogany bar, with its brass fixtures, was backed by shelves of bottles of whiskey, gin, rum and brandy. They were reflected in huge mirrors which seemed to magnify the size of the gambling joint. 'Some place you got here.'

A bar-tender, his hair slicked back, in an apron and shirt sleeves, gave the dusty drifter the once over. 'Yeah. What's your poison?'

'I'll have one of them Kansan steam beers.'

Anderson put a weather-faded boot-toe on the foot rail. 'Bet this place is packed-out in the season, ain't it? You must make a fortune.'

The 'keep flicked foam from the glass with a spatula and slid it along to his customer's ready hand. 'You could say. Plenty fortunes lost, too. One sucker last summer gambled away his whole herd of cows.'

'You don't say? Who owns this joint?'

'Mr Atkinson. He's away East right now.'

'Must be the richest man in town.'

'You joking? What about Jake Karatovsky? Started off selling boots, hats, gents' suits and denim work clothes out of a big corn bin. Soon as stuff came in he sold it on at two hundred per cent mark-up. Owns two stores now. The whores don't do too badly for 'emselves, either.'

'Yeah?' Anderson enquired innocently. 'Where do they hang out?'

'In what they call the Devil's Addition. Some of these God-worshipping settlers' wives didn't like seeing 'em walking the streets so they've been banished to a red-light district half a mile away down the trail. Mind you, it's as difficult keeping them frisky gals caged up as it is keeping the longhorns in their pens.'

'Yep.' Anderson downed his beer and gave his flicker of a grin. 'I can guess. So, who else is on the make?'

'Mister!' the 'keep whooped. 'The hypocrites who run this town tut-tut about the wild goings on, but they're the first to capitalize. They squeeze the farm-

17

ers and settlers harder than the Texan cowboys.'

He looked about him and lowered his voice. 'You're the feller who killed Bloody Bob, aincha? Seen you in The Longhorn. You were talkin' to the mayor. That fat banker's grabbing and selling land as fast as he can, charging farmers thirty to sixty per cent on loans. He's got a finger in every pie.'

'Yeah? He offered me the job of city marshal.'

The 'keep gave a scoffing laugh as he arranged a pile of glasses. 'Did he say what happened to our other two?'

'No. What did?'

'Bear River Tom could handle himself in a fight, but he made the mistake of going unarmed. They found him with his head chopped off.'

Anderson grunted. 'Nasty.'

'So they got Hickok. Wild Bill. But he was *too* wild. He shot a fellow officer in a fracas. The town committee threw him out. Anyway, they couldn't afford the hundred fifty a month they were paying him, not in off-season.'

'That's three times more than Hooson offered me.'

'See!' the 'keep grinned. 'Told ya you have to watch him.'

Anderson tossed down a quarter for the beer, boom town price, he guessed, and took a stroll along to the stockyards and railway depot. He passed an imposing three-storey, eighty-room hotel named, perhaps ironically, the Drovers' Cottage – some cottage – built by the founder of the town, Joe McCoy. No doubt cattle barons and wheeler-dealers sat out on its spacious covered veranda in the summer, but it didn't look the kind of place he could afford to stay just yet.

He paid three bits for a hole in the wall at Ma Riley's rooming-house, a warren of narrow plank rooms furnished with iron beds which no doubt, soon enough, would be filled to the brim with raucous Texan cowhands whooping it up when they arrived with the herds. It was practically empty now, so he dumped his saddle-bags, rifle and blanket roll, and went to get the stubble scraped from his lean cheeks at the barber shop.

Maybe, he thought, as he looked at his wolfish reflection in the glass, there were possibilities to cut into some of this town's profits.

'Hooson, I been thinking about your offer.' He found the mayor behind his grille at the bank. 'I ain't putting my life on the line for chicken feed. A hundred a month's my price. But I want a month in advance. I'm short of cash.'

'This is most unusual, Mr Anderson,' the mayor blustered. 'I'll have to discuss it with the town committee. I'm afraid seventy's the most we could go to.'

'You paid Hickok a hundred and fifty.'

'Somebody's been talking, have they?' The mayor gave his oily smile. 'But you're not Hickok.'

'True. But I figure I could handle the job. It ain't something a man takes on lightly. Make it eighty. If you want me, hand it over now or I ride on out tonight.'

'You drive a hard bargain.'

'You won't regret it,' Anderson said, patting the

grip of his revolver. 'Let's hope neither will I.'

'Right.' The mayor counted out the cash, slid it through the grille with a metal star. 'Sign this receipt. You'll be needing the badge. Meet me in the morning, seven sharp. I'll show you the ropes.'

Anderson tucked the roll of greenbacks in his pocket and gave his grim, lean-jawed grin. 'That'll be interestin', I'm sure.'

He groaned as a slatternly maid pushed into his room the next morning with a jug of hot water and placed it on the wash bowl. 'What time is it?'

'Six-thirty.'

'Right.' He stuck his hat on his head, rolled out of the cot, and pulled on his boots. 'I'd better go see what Fatso's got to say.'

He had passed the evening before in a poker game, calling it quits at two in the morning. He counted his roll of greenbacks. Half his month's wage had been eaten away. 'Christ! I ain't the greatest poker player in the world.'

Hooson was waiting to unlock the jailhouse. 'You've got a chance to prove yourself. There's been a robbery. The tinsmith, Wallace Peacock, found his stable broken into this morning, his wagon and pair gone.'

'Jeez, what am I s'posed to do?'

'Go after 'em. He checked the stable at ten last night, so it was probably taken about midnight.'

'So they, or he, or whoever it was, has got an eight-hour lead on me,' Anderson protested. 'How do I know which way they gawn?'

'Probably south towards the Indian nations. Once over the line they'll be in federal jurisdiction so you better move fast.'

'I had a late night,' Anderson muttered. 'Need a good strong coffee first. What do I do when I catch 'em?'

The mayor shrugged his fleshy shoulders and gave him a wide-eyed stare. 'That's up to you. They got into the shop, rifled the till, took a hundred and thirty-seven dollars. All Mr Peacock wants is the return of his property. He's got urgent deliveries to make.'

Hooson bustled about, flicking through a pile of court forms, Wanted notices, log books, tossing the keys of the three cells on to a desk. 'I'll explain your other duties when you get back.'

'Let's get this straight: you tellin' me you ain't bothered whether I bring in a prisoner or not?'

'Well, they generally hang horse-thieves in these parts.' The mayor rubbed his pudgy hands. 'Depends whether you want a lot of paperwork and enjoy serving criminals breakfast in bed. It's your decision. You're the marshal now.'

'Yeah, so it seems.' Anderson locked up, put the key in his pocket, and sauntered over to The Longhorn. 'Morning Jim,' he called to the boy. 'My usual.' He leaned on the bar and stared up at the doleful skull of a longhorn on the wall. 'Yeah, that's about how I feel, too.'

The spiked coffee revived him. 'Some damn fool stole the tinsmith's wagon. I gotta go after him. I'm your new marshal, didja know? More fool me. Guess

I'd better pin on my badge to make it legal.'

The bald-headed owner of the billiards hall, Hyram Hunnisegger, was standing further along the bar. 'That must be them two I seen driving Peacock's wagon outa town about one when I was locking up. Two *hombres* I didn't recognize. One a black. Thought somebody's stove mighta collapsed and they was workin' overtime. Odd, now I think about it.'

'Whichaway was they headed?'

'On the trail south.'

'Yeah, well, next time maybe you could tell me earlier.'

'Didn't know we had a new marshal.'

'You know now,' Anderson gritted out, and pointed at his coffee mug for another shot of whiskey. 'Jim, can you make me up a packet of grub to eat while I ride?'

'Sure, Marshal. Anythang you need.'

Anderson's grey mare was a deep-chested quarter horse built for endurance, She went at a steady lope from mid-morning to sundown without complaint. Overnight rain made the wagon tracks easily visible. They left the main trail and seemed to be following the Smoky Hill river, possibly heading for Big Bend. He paused for rest once, brewing up coffee and chewing the ham in half a loaf Jim had put together. He let the mare drink very sparsely and pushed on. He needed to cut this chase short before these two disappeared into some hidey-hole.

It was green, wooded, rolling countryside, and, as the last rays of the sun flickered on the western horizon, Anderson figured he must have come forty miles and would have to call it a day. Then he saw the flicker of a campsite up ahead. 'Got 'em,' he said.

He ground-hitched the mare and went ahead on foot clutching the Creedmore across his chest. It was the finest rifle Remington had ever produced, powerful and accurate at long range. He crept closer and saw the silhouettes in the dusk of two men sitting on a fallen tree, crouched over a fire, enjoying their evening meal. The wagon and two horses were nearby.

'Grab air,' he shouted, 'unless you want your spines shattered.'

They both froze, then one rose and slowly turned. It must have been the black guy because all Anderson could see were the whites of his eyes. He aimed just above, punched out a powerful .44-.100 slug which sent his straw hat spinning. 'The next one's 'tween your eyes,' he growled.

It had the desired effect. Anderson approached as both men held their hands high. 'I ain't in no mood to argue, boys. You've led me a merry chase. Where's that hundred and what was it, thirty-seven dollars, you stole? Come on, dough up.'

'Whatcha gonna do with us?' the black fellow whined as he dug out his share. 'They'll lynch us you take us back.'

'Maybe I oughta save them the bother,' Anderson grunted.

He disarmed them, and tossed their weapons on to Peacock's wagon, the name enscrolled on its sides for all to see. 'But I left my rope back with my hoss.' He counted the cash. 'Correct,' he said. 'Don't look like

I'm gonna git much outa this for myself. Is that rabbit stew you got there? Smells good. Dish me up a good plateful, boys. Then we'll call it quits. You can go on your way.'

He made them squat on the damp ground while he sat on the log, the rifle propped by his side, and munched at a rabbit leg with relish. 'A drop of your coffee would be nice.'

When he was full, he ordered them to harness the pair back in the rig. 'I wouldn't advise you to come after me or show your faces in Abilene again, boys. You been lucky this time.'

'You cain't leave us here without horses or guns,' the older white ruffian groaned. 'It ain't right.'

'You'll soon find a coupla more hosses to thieve. So long, boys. Have a nice walk.' Anderson urged the tired pair in the wagon traces out of the campsite. 'Thanks for the stew.'

He hitched the grey at the back and drove five miles through the dark before hauling in the horses, and bedding down in the back of the wagon. 'Them two varmints ain't gonna bother us none,' he muttered, as he watched the moon rise. 'We'll take it easy back to town. Twenty miles a day will be fast enough. Do a bit of fishing on the way. We're gittin' paid for it. Wonder how much I can charge expenses?'

With such thoughts the new marshal fell into a deep sleep and knew no more until he woke with the sun in his eyes. Well, he thought, my first mission accomplished. But he knew his future assignments were not all going to be so easy.

THREE

When the hotshot promoter Joe McCoy first saw Abilene five years before it was a handful of log huts servicing buffalo hunters, a small halt on the rail line out on the trackless prairie. He decided it would be the ideal spot to build stockyards as the main market for herds of Texan longhorns being driven north. So, with not a cow yet in sight, he grabbed 250 key acres of land, imported stout lumber from Missouri to construct pens for as many as 3,000 bawling long-horns, and persuaded the Kansas Pacific railroad company to install switches and sidings and to carry cattle at five dollars a carload. He built liveries, barns, stables, weighing scales, offices and the magnificent Drovers' Cottage hotel where deals could be done, drummed up business for beeves in New York and Chicago, and waited for trail herds to arrive.

By now, 1872, Abilene was reaching bustling matu-rity as a pioneer cattle town. But the arrival each summer of hordes of hard-drinking, fast-shooting Texans, plus hundreds of whores, gamblers, conmen and drifting ne'er-do-wells in their wake was not to everyone's liking. 'Hell is now in session,' as Aaron Cox, the editor of *The Abilene Clarion*, put it.

Dentists, doctors, land agents, lawyers, dry goods merchants and settlers seeking a new life had flocked to the new town. A stone schoolhouse was being built alongside a second church, and now voices were being raised with pious horror at the sound of gunfights throughout the night, screams and laughter and the wanton behaviour of young hussies, some not over sixteen, drinking whiskey, smoking cigars, cursing and misbehaving lewdly.

'People in this town got a bad case of the respectables,' Mayor Hooson told the marshal when he returned. 'They don't see that it's the Texans who lay our golden eggs. Where would we be without 'em?'

Anderson was taking a drink in The Longhorn, well pleased with the twenty dollars reward Wallace Peacock had parted with for the return of his cash and wagon. 'Sounds to me like a recipe for trouble,' he muttered.

'It is. The town committee has come up with all kind of laws banning prostitution, underage drinking, and the carrying of firearms in the streets,' the mayor mused. 'It will be up to you to implement them.'

'I had an idea there might be a catch to it when you offered me this job,' Anderson drawled. 'Just how am I supposed to do that?'

'We'll be employing a deputy in the season to help you out,' Hooson responded hurriedly. 'So, what did you do with those two miscreants?'

Anderson's flinty eyes met the mayor's watery blue ones. 'I dealt with 'em,' he grunted.

'You've done well so far,' Hooson remarked, smirking as he passed a copy of *Tthe Abilene Clarion* to the marshal. 'You've made the headlines. This is just what we need, the support of the Press.'

Anderson put his drink aside and studied the news item.

Abilene has a new marshal, Henry 'Hank' Anderson, who appears to be quick on the trigger. He has already brought an end to the notorious career of Bloody Bob Brown, and successfully pursued two thieves who made off with Mr Peacock's wagon, horses and shop takings. The marshal trailed them 200 miles south and, after an exchange of leaden compliments, returned safely with the stolen items.

Anderson gave a wry smile because it seemed they believed his slight exaggeration, and read on.

Although I am yet to meet the new marshal, I am reliably informed that he hails from Missouri and this lean six-footer looks like he knows what he's about. It seems he has already gained the entire confidence of the mayor and leading citizens. Time, of course, will tell, but any gun-crazy Texans might be well advised to take care in future: we have a capable law officer ready and waiting for them.

'Jeez,' Anderson growled. 'What's he have to write that horse manure fer? Now every pistol-packing dude

27

in the county's gonna come lookin' fer me. Could you tell your esteemed editor I would welcome no more publicity?'

'You can tell him yourself,' the mayor replied. 'We'll go across and I'll interdooce ya.' He added, by way of inducement, 'He's got a real humdinger of a daughter, Jane Cox.'

'Is that her full name?' the marshal muttered, 'or an intimation of what she might git up to?'

Hooson frowned at him. 'I wouldn't try anything with Jane. She's a real blue-stocking, a reg'lar church-goer, an' the apple of her daddy's eye. Her father's very protective.'

'Ain't they all?' Anderson reached for his hat. 'The ones I meet, that is.'

But as they made their way along the sidewalk they met a *real* goodlooker, Lizzie Upstone. In a sunbonnet and ankle-length white cotton dress, a basket of shopping on her arm, her blue eyes lit up at the sight of the marshal.

'Hello, Lizzie,' the mayor greeted. 'Have you been introduced to Mr Anderson, our new lawman, yet?'

'No,' the girl gushed, in a husky whisper, 'but I've been longing to thank you in person, Mr Anderson, for saving my life.'

Anderson gripped her proffered hand, dainty and warm to his touch. 'Dunno about your life, Lizzie, it was your virtue I was more worried about. Let's hope it's still intact.'

A blush began at the girl's temples and spread to the rest of her heart-shaped face as she stammered, 'I want to thank you, anyway.' She tried to withdraw her fingers but the marshal was holding tight.

'Ya know, Lizzie.' A smile flickered across his jaws. 'You remind me of a gal I once knew in Missouri. She was sweet, innocent, naïve and damn pretty, just like you.'

The girl stared at him with her animated blue eyes. 'Really?'

'Yeah, sure thang.' Anderson let slip her hand. 'Stay that way, will ya?'

'I'll try, sir,' Lizzie gasped.

Anderson gave a caustic laugh. 'I was only fifteen at the time. Her daddy didn't like me, mainly on account of I was the orphan boy they'd taken in. That, of course, meant being his free white slave.'

'Come along, Marshal,' Hooson put in, grabbing his arm. 'We haven't got time to listen to your life story.'

'No, I guess you ain't. Don't know why I'm tellin' y'all this.' Anderson gave a rueful grin. 'So long, Lizzie. See ya around.'

The girl stood and watched them go as the mayor lectured, 'I hope you're not going to behave like that to every girl in the town.'

'Listen, Hooson,' the marshal said, jerking his arm free. 'I'll behave just the hell how I like. Your only interest in me is whether I do my job right. And if I don't you and your committee can go to blazes for all I care.'

'OK, Marshal, don't get het up,' Hooson blustered. 'All I'm saying is our lawman needs to act with a little decorum. That gal's under age so keep your hands off her. You start skirt-chasing all over town and you're not going to be very popular with the menfolk.'

'I was just passing the time of day with the girl. I ain't after her. And I ain't aiming to be popular,' Anderson growled. 'That's the last thing I want to be especially with people of your ilk.

'What do you mean by that?'

'I mean profiteers and swindlers, men who sit in their pew on Sundays chanting their prayers and pretending to be righteous businessmen.'

'Come, come, Marshal.' The mayor had one hand on the door of *The Clarion* office, about to enter. 'We all have to make a living. No need to be so surly. I trust you'll be polite to Miss Cox.'

'I'll try.' The marshal gave a grin as he spotted a young woman standing behind a tall desk inside. 'But I cain't promise anythang.'

Jane Cox had a severe, old-fashioned look, typical of this buttoned-up Victorian age, what folks might call a 'blue nose', her brown hair scooped back tightly into a bun at the back of her long-jawed face. But her up-turned smile when she saw the visitors imparted a certain sparkle.

'It's a pleasure to meet you, Marshal.' She offered her hand to Anderson. 'You've already made quite an impression on my father although it's only hearsay.' Her fingers were icy cold and she quickly removed them from his horny-handed grasp, fluttering them in an agitated manner.

'So I've read.'

'Come in and meet him.'

'Yeah, I'd like to.' Anderson followed her through to the print room, admiring her jaunty *derrière* beneath a tight, pleated skirt.

An employee in an apron was standing before slanted cases of lead type, another hammering with a mallet at a form, locking it and applying ink with a roller. A boy was slicing up sheets of paper and there was a general air of activity.

Pride of place was taken by a sturdy Washington hand press, its workings not much changed since Gutenberg's original of the fifteenth century. Jane explained how it worked, placing a paper sheet on a hinged wooden tympan, folding it down over the form of type, then sliding the bed bearing the form beneath the big platen. She tugged at a lever pressing the platen down to form an impression.

'There's the fresh-printed page,' she exclaimed, removing it with a flourish to show him. 'This is just an advertising bill, of course. As well as being a newspaper office we're a jobbing printer's.'

'So if you need any Wanted posters turning out,' the major put in, 'this is the place to come.'

'Yes, I'm *impressed*.' the marshal grinned. 'Geddit?'

Like England's Victoria, Jane was not amused. 'This way,' she said, leading them to a back office of the wooden building where a gaunt-jowled fellow with wild grey hair was behind a desk piled with books, papers, letters and other oddments. He peered up over his spectacles, quill in hand. 'Ah, the marshal,' he cried. 'Good to see you. Jane, move that junk off that chair. Take a seat, Mr Anderson, or may I call you Hank?'

'You can call me what you like as long as it's not in print. To be frank, I've a complaint about that piece you wrote about me, Mr Cox. You no doubt meant well, but I'm allergic to seeing details of my personal life bandied about for all to behold. So I'd be glad if you'd desist in future.'

'*Desist?* My dear man,' Aaron Cox protested, waving his pen about, 'you can't gag a free press. People have a right to know what their new marshal is like as a man. If you consider the piece over-adulatory you may have a point. But be assured that if you should ever fail in your duties mine will be the first voice to say so.'

'Yeah, well, I just want to have a go at this job in my own fashion, and I don't see how shining a light on my activities is going to help any.'

'We have to cover crime and court proceedings,' Jane Cox cried. 'That's *our* duty. Your name is bound to come up quite frequently. As long as we do so in an honest, professional manner I don't see what your gripe is.'

Hooson tried to smooth the troubled waters. 'Hank's just very modest by nature. He's not used to such publicity.'

'I don't like it,' Anderson growled, 'and I don't wan' it. Thass all I got to say.'

'I'm sorry you feel this way,' Aaron Cox remarked, as the marshal got up to leave. 'I was reporting what I had heard. I had hoped we could have a friendly discussion about your plans for the future—'

'That's OK,' Anderson replied, as he held open the door for Jane to squeeze past him. 'I'll be glad to git friendly with y'all any other day so long as you abide by my request.'

The newspaper editor stared after them, drop-jawed, as his daughter showed the marshal out. 'Who's that young man think he is? He's got a chip on his shoulder the size of Mount Rushmore.'

'I guess he can't help that,' Hoosen soothed. 'He comes from Missouri. That's the way they are.'

'It seems to me you've fished up a queer one to protect us, Clarence,' Cox muttered. 'Strikes me our marshal might have swum in murky waters.'

'Don't go stirring things up, Aaron,' the mayor beseeched him. 'He's the best man for a dirty job. Let's give him a chance, shall we?'

'He seems a decent sort, if a bit surly,' Jane remarked when she returned. 'But why is he so public-ity shy?'

'Isn't it obvious? He must have something to hide. Perhaps we ought to dig a bit deeper into Mr Anderson's past. It might well surprise us. In the meantime, my dear, I advise you to treat him with caution. I mean, don't get too friendly.'

'One thing's for sure,' Jane cried. 'He's not going to restrict my reporting activities. The cheek of the man!'

FOUR

'I guess I shouldn't have ruffled their feathers,' the marshal muttered to himself as he poured coffee from a pot on the stove. 'Nor should I have mentioned Missouri to that barman, Jim. He musta been talkin'.'

He sank into a swivel chair putting his boots up on his desk. 'This ain't a bad li'l number. I don't partic'larly want to move on.'

No, he was tired of drifting. He had planned to get himself a job maybe 'riding shotgun' in a gambling joint, put some cash aside, look around for a nice piece of land to settle on, run a few cows and breed horses, get a dog, or even a wife, live in peace for once in his life. Or was that impossible, a pipe dream?

Suddenly he was town marshal. It was ironic. For the past seven years he had been hard riding, fighting, shooting. Yes, he had done his share of killing, robbing, pillaging, setting homes to the flames. He had hoped he could put it behind him. But could a man ever escape his past? And now he had aroused the suspicions of Cox. 'Why the hell didn't I give them

34

a different name, an alias?' he wondered.

Henry Anderson was the name they had given him at the St Louis orphanage. He had no idea who his parents were. When he was eleven years old a man had arrived and offered to adopt him, give him a home. Some home! That mean-faced farmer worked him from dawn to dusk like one of his animals, hauling out stumps, ploughing, hewing wood, fetching water, feeding the pigs. He had supper in the kitchen of their cabin at the family table, but was regarded askance, an outsider, and sent every night to go sleep in the stable. Out there in the darkness, in snow, sleet or hail, he had cursed Old Man Somers and his down-trodden wife, vowed to get even with them one day.

Their only child, Rose, was their opposite in nature. Dreamy, languorous, she sought the good in everyone, loved all God's creatures, wouldn't even eat meat since first seeing a cow slaughtered and hearing hogs have their throats cut. Brow-beaten by her parents, she was forbidden to speak to the boy, but cast him sidelong glances, sought him out when she could.

Their land was in a desolate part of Missouri, the nearest town Sedalia, miles away. He and Rose began to live a secret life of their own. In the summer she would wander bare-foot through the meadows collecting flowers, show him, as he worked, frogs or butterflies she had found. As they grew older she would sneak into the barn after she was supposed to be abed, read to him from some book of poems. Soon they began to hold hands, to kiss, and when they were both fourteen the inevitable happened, *he did it to her*, as they say.

They had sworn to love each other for ever, and maybe Hank had meant to honour that vow. But it was a time of War between the States. One day a band of 400 rebels rode into the farm, not regular troops, but a bunch of bloodthirsty guerillas led by a cold-hearted psychopath called Captain William Quantrill. 'If you're not with us, you're against us.' Anderson could still recall the words ringing out, the horror on Rose's face as Quantrill pointed at him and shouted, 'We're taking the boy. He must fight for the cause.'

Somers stood before his cabin door protesting, perhaps more because of his pigs being killed, his cows driven off, his kitchen looted. Quantrill pointed a revolver at the farmer and shot him down. 'Give him a horse,' he said, nodding at the youth. Anderson was made to mount up and follow them. He rode with them for the rest of the war and became almost as wild and battle-hardened as the worst.

The fighting on the borders of Missouri and Kansas was perhaps the most bitter of the war, reaching its apogée at the small town of Lawrence in '64. Quantrill was out of control, ordering that every male of arms-bearing age be killed. They executed the army garrison and civilians in twos, roped back to back, so one bullet would suffice. One hundred and fifty men, women and children were massacred that day.

Hank Anderson had been sickened by it, but what could he do? If he had refused orders he would have been shot, too. Men like Jesse James and his brother, Frank, and the Younger brothers, were as merciless as Quantrill. When Jefferson Davis, President of the

Confederacy, denounced them they paid no heed. They rode on, more intent on plunder, on filling their own pockets, than fighting for the 'sacred Southern cause'.

Quantrill had been commissioned as a captain of partisan rangers and his border ruffians mustered into the Confederate Army. But by the end of the war, after Quantrill had been shot dead in a raid, his guerillas were regarded as little more than outlaws by both sides.

Hank remembered how Jesse and the boys hung around in wooded country debating whether to surrender. They had been offered safe conduct if they rode into a Union camp down in the valley and took the oath of allegiance.

Jesse, Hank and some others had been the first to go down. Hank saw a bunch of hated Kansan Red Legs – so-named for their red gaiters – lined up awaiting them. The Rebs were ordered to lay down their arms. As they did so the youth noticed two Red Legs on the back of a wagon. Some instinct warned him to scream out, 'It's a trap!' The canvas cover of a Gatling gun was pulled aside and its deathly stutter rattled out. His comrades fell in their death throes.

Anderson had run to leap on a horse, snatching its reins, kicking it away, riding low and fast for the woods as bullets whistled over his head. He and Jesse James were the only ones to survive that day.

Jesse had returned to Missouri, but Anderson had kept on riding, after meeting up with a few of the boys, heading further and further away into the south-west. They had drifted through New Mexico, crossing the

Rio Grande, reaching Silver City. He had hoped he could go straight, maybe get rich in the silver mines. But, nineteen by now, he was a hothead and got into some trouble over cards, shooting down a gambling man. An outlaw again, for three years he rode with the notorious Wilcox gang, rustling cattle, stealing horses, holding up travellers and stage coaches in that rugged mountainous territory. When Bob Wilcox was killed in a bank raid that went bad at Socorro on the Rio Grande, Hank knew it was time to get out.

When the Governor of New Mexico at Santa Fe offered the remnants of the Wilcox gang a free pardon on condition they quit the territory, Hank decided to do just that. Sure they had been wild, exciting times, but he was getting older, seeing some sense, and he grabbed at the chance to reform.

Maybe he should have gone further west to Arizona, or California, but no, something drew him back towards Kansas. 'I was a fool to come back,' he mused. 'Folks round here ain't likely to forgive and forget. Lawrence is only a hundred and fifty miles east of here. They are bound to find out I was there.'

If they did, the marshal guessed he would just have to brazen it out. Why, too, had he spoken out about Rose· today? It was the first time he had ever mentioned her name to anyone. Could it be he had a hankering to see her again?

'That's another fool idea,' he muttered. 'We were just kids. That episode was near on ten years ago. She'll be a married woman by now. It's no good raking up the past. It's best forgotten.'

The next morning Hank was engaged in the most
important task of the week for journalists, police
officers, and politicians – George Washington
himself was a dab hand at it – writing out an inven-
tive expenses chit to present to the mayor for
approval. He had told a few little white lies about his
first assignment, saying that he had trailed the
wagon thieves for three days covering 300 miles. At
ten cents a mile that added up to thirty dollars. He
had, he said, engaged those two bad men in an hour-
long gun battle and had blasted a couple of holes in
the wagon side to prove so. His allowance for ammu-
nition would be . . . hmm . . . let's see . . . he licked
his pencil deep in thought as he did his sums. Well,
he might have turned over a new leaf, but no man
was completely honest, except a fool, was he? It was
all in a good cause, for what he termed his 'ranch
fund'. Every little helped. If he could stay out of
poker games one of these days he'd have enough in
his pot to buy and stock a small spread.

He was disturbed in his calculations by the jingle of
harness and the sound of numerous hoofs thudding
the hard mud street outside his office. Glancing
through the barred window he saw a company of US
cavalry riding in. Old habits died hard. He tensed and
his hand went to the butt of his Remington. It was the
imbued instinct of a former Reb.

'Hey, man,' he crooned. 'I'm on their side now. I
better go see what they want.'

In their navy-blue uniforms, sabres hanging from their hips, they had drawn in before The Longhorn and were parleying with young Jim, who had come out on to the sidewalk. A moustachioed sergeant appeared to be in charge.

'What's the trouble?' Anderson asked, as he joined Jim.

'No trouble, Marshal,' the sergeant called. 'We're on our way to Fort Dodge. Just looking for a bit of rest and recreation, that's all.'

'I told 'em to go on down to the Devil's Addition,' Jim said. 'We might have whiskey but we don't have no wimmin in here.'

'Yeah, true. It's just a short way down the trail,' Anderson sang out. 'Have a good time, boys. Be nice to the gals and they'll be nice to you.'

The sergeant saluted lazily and led his men away at a fast clip, the colour of the 7th Cavalry fluttering in the breeze.

'They say there's trouble brewing with the Sioux,' Jim cried out. 'It's good to know the army's here to protect us.'

'Yeah,' Anderson drawled, 'as long as that's what they do do.'

He had to go to a meeting of the town committee, then tack up on suitable walls and telegraph poles copies of numerous restrictive bye-laws they had come up with. 'What a lot of stuffed shirts,' Anderson muttered. 'Still, I s'pose they're paying my wages.'

About five o'clock he decided to go take a look at how the soldier boys were getting on. He left his

Creedmore in the rack and the mare in the stable and strolled down that way on foot. As he got nearer the hoots of drunken celebration grew louder and almost deafening as he stepped into the smoky atmosphere of Rosy Joe's.

Troopers were jam packed along the bar or sprawled on chairs, divested of their jackets and sabres, bottles of hooch in their fists, cheroots clamped in teeth, playing cards, shouting or raucously singing along to 'Pop Goes the Weasel', or similar refrains pounded out by an old guy on an out-of-tune piano.

Some of the soldiers had half-dressed *filles-de-joie* sat on their laps, or, with a whoop, would drag one up the rickety staircase to the bedrooms above. Rosy Joe, in his frock coat and Lincoln hat, was busy behind the bar helping deal with this unexpected trade.

Anderson found a space at the far end. He saw now how the saloon-keeper had earned his soubriquet. His face and fleshy nose pitted with 'grog blossoms', was a glorious bouquet to 'the Goddess of Rum'. Some called him Rosy *Nose* Joe behind his back. Reknowned for his temper, Joe would crack rowdy drinkers craniums with his billy stick if so inclined.

'Whadda ya want, Marshal?' Joe asked, in his tough manner. 'You ain't got no jurisdiction here. You're out of city limits.'

Anderson nodded. 'Maybe. How's it going?'

'Wonderful. Ain't been so busy in months.' Joe

plonked a whiskey bottle and tumbler before the lawman. 'Help yourself.'

The marshal half-filled the half-pint tumbler and took a tentative gulp of the fiery potion. It was true that the town laws regarding prostitution and drinking did not apply down here. But if there was any other mayhem, he might be forced to intervene. Apart from the horrendous racket most of the troopers seemed to be behaving reasonably.

Nearby, at a little desk built into the bar, sat Joe's woman, Big Kate, the saloon madame, her large frame and massive bosom encased in a girlie, candy-striped dress. She was sporting numerous rings, bracelets and a flashy necklace, her mass of hennaed red hair coiled and piled on top of her head. On her lap was a little Mexican Chihuahua. Occasionally she would exchange one of her whorehouse tokens for a drunken soldier's cash and indicate to one of her soiled doves to attend to him. 'Just look at these sweet li'l soldier boys enjoyin' 'emselves!' she exclaimed, winking at the marshal. 'Ain't it a pretty sight?'

As he eyed Kate, 'mutton dressed as lamb' came into Anderson's mind, and he was amused to see that one of the younger-looking troopers obviously had a taste for the older woman for he appeared to be propositioning her.

'I ain't for sale, junior,' Kate smirked, her red lips glistening about her yellowed teeth. 'Find another playmate.'

But the lad wasn't satisfied, arguing vociferously,

pushing past the marshal and grabbing hold of Rosy Joe's arm.

'Hey, mister,' he shouted. 'She said iffen I bought this token I could have any dame in the house. Waal, I want *her*. I've taken a fancy to them tits.'

'Yeah?' Joe stood with a glass in his hand studying the soldier. 'You're quite right, Sonny Jim. Hey, Kate, this lad may be going into battle against the Sioux any day soon. He's a hero. Get up them stairs with him.'

The lapdog started a shrill yapping as Kate protested. She screamed as Joe gave her a hefty back-hander across the jaw, nearly knocking her off her stool. 'You lazy sow, think I keep you to sit on your arse all day? All the gals are working their socks off so you better, too.'

Big Kate quickly backed out of the bar, caught hold of the soldier. 'Come on then, you li'l squirt, let's see what you're made of.'

Joe kicked the yapping lapdog from under his feet and leered, ruefully, at Anderson. 'She's a good woman, just needs a firm hand now and again. Dogs, wimmin, hosses, that's the only language they understand, ain't that so, Marshal?'

He tried to wave away payment but Anderson shrugged, slapped down a quarter, and headed for the door. Outside it was getting dusk and some of the troopers were nosing into the row of stall-like cribs between the two saloons, but most had no occupants at this time of the year.

Hank followed a couple of the soldiers, unsteady on

their feet, into the Last or First Chance, which harboured a similar scene of dissolution. The strapping Norwegian who presided, Red Ingmarson, was looking pleased with himself, too. A mass of ginger curls about his glowing face fell to his shoulders and ran into his pointed beard. A revolver was stuck in a stout leather belt about his barrel of a belly. 'How yah, Marshal?' he bellowed, plonking a whiskey bottle before him. 'Velcome to my house. You wanna do businness viv me?'

'What kinda business?'

'Money business. You come here every night, *ja*? Any trouble you take care for me. I pay fifty a week.'

'You wanna buy my services?'

'*Ja*, but you have nothink to do wiv that Rosy Joe. That man, his head so big, he think he own this town. You be my man, huh, Marshal?'

'Nope. I ain't takin' sides. What you do with gals an' gambling is your business. But if there's any killings I'm gonna have to arrest the perpetrator.'

'Oh, *ja*?' Ingmarson wailed. 'Too bad.'

The sergeant of cavalry lurched towards them. Without his hat he was as bald as a billiard ball, the danglers of his moustache drooping to his yellow bandanna. He looked a tad drunk by now, like most of his men.

'Hi, thar, Marshal,' he slurred. 'What brings you here? Gonna wet ya whistle or dip yur wick?'

'Just keepin' an eye on things. When you moving out?'

'When I say so and when we've had enough.'

'Like tonight?'

'Sure, like tonight. Everythang's under control.' But as he spoke there was a deafening gunshot from a few yards away.

'Get away from me!' a girl called Milly McGhee screamed. 'I ain't got your money.'

Taken by surprise, like everybody else, Anderson could only glimpse through the crowd a female arm brandishing a smoking revolver. Her hand was gripped by those of a soldier. Another explosion and a bullet ripped through the ceiling. Another scream from upstairs.

'Give me the gun,' the trooper shouted, 'you thievin', pox-riddled whore.'

Anderson hauled men aside to get a better look, his Remington raised and cocked for action. The trooper was grappling with Milly for the pistol. He swung her arm down. The gun went off again and a bullet smashed into her upper thigh.

Red, too, now came up from behind the bar with his six-shooter and began blasting bullets indiscriminately at the soldiers in the saloon.

There were more agonized cries as one trooper caught lead in the boot, penetrating his shin, making him howl. Red's second slug hit a corporal in the shoulder, sending him spinning, crashing back onto a table.

Bedlam ensued as girls screamed and soldiers scrambled to avoid the flying lead.

The marshal fired at Red, severing his trigger finger, and making him drop the weapon like a red-hot coal. Then Anderson grabbed hold of the offending trooper by the scruff of his neck, dragged him back towards the bar to act as a shield, and stuck the Remington's barrel into his ear.

'Drop the gun,' he hissed, and shouted, 'Hold it, everybody. That's enough bloodshed for tonight. There's three down and another upstairs by the sound of things. Back off, boys. Get outa this saloon or your pal here gits it through the brain – if he's got one.'

The moustachioed sergeant lurched drunkenly to the front, raising his carbine. 'Do as the marshal says, men. Corporal Thompson looks in a bad way. Somebody go get the doc.'

Red stood staring at the stump of his finger, holding it aloft to staunch the blood amid obscene threats hurled at him as to what the troopers planned to do to him. But gradually they dispersed to join others of their ranks outside.

'Flossie's got it through the throat,' a prostitute shrieked from the top of the stairs. 'Somebody help.'

'Aw, shee-it,' Anderson groaned, keeping hold of the soldier. 'Now hear what you done.'

'It weren't me,' the soldier boy said, pointing to the girl on the floor with blood seeping from her thigh. 'It was Milly. I was trying to stop her.'

'I'll take him, Marshal.' The sergeant beckoned Anderson to hand his prisoner over. 'Private Grimes will be dealt with by court martial.'

'Nope,' Anderson said. 'He ain't going nowhere except my jail.'

'Don't be a fool, Marshal. That's asking for more

trouble. My boys are all fired up. It's gonna be hard enough getting 'em to go back to camp as it is.'

'I ain't a fool. It's you damn fools who've caused this. You just git your men outa town double quick.'

The sergeant had his carbine half-raised, his finger on the trigger. 'You wouldn't blow his head off. It's a bluff.'

Anderson gave a caustic grin. 'Try me.'

The sergeant snarled, threateningly. 'This ain't the end of it. We'll be back.'

It was at this point that Jane Cox drove a spirited chestnut galloping down the street, Doc Rosen hanging on beside her on the high-wheeled buggy.

'How did it happen?' she asked, as they rushed into the First or Last Chance.

Anderson was securing his prisoner's wrist's behind him with handcuffs. 'This'n and her on the floor were fighting for a gun. Then it all accelerated. I'll tell ya later. I'm kinda busy right now.'

Eventually, as the doctor treated the wounded, removing slugs, one from Milly McGhee's thigh, others from Flossie Love's throat, the corporal's shoulder and the soldier's shin, patching them all up, and Red too, calm reigned. The sergeant had rounded up his men from both establishments and they were ready to ride, but he insisted that the corporal and wounded squaddie be carried out and put on their horses. As the company cantered away back to their camp a couple of miles out of town, one of the troopers shouted, 'Keep your chin up, Grimes. We ain't gonna forget this.'

'Come on,' Anderson growled, frog-marching the trooper up the trail back to the jail. 'Think yourself lucky I didn't shoot you down like the mad dog that y'are, only I'm on a kinda love-thy-neighbour thing at the moment.'

FIVE

ran *The Clarion*'s banner headline the next morning.

Two women and two soldiers badly wounded, said the sub-head. *The soldiers' comrades highly indignant. Lively times expected.*

Once again an Abilene saloon weltered in blood as gunshots were exchanged wildly and two females not yet out of their teens learned the folly of their sinful ways, it was stated.

The girls had been tippling, dancing, whoring and misbehaving themselves with a company of Union cavalry in Ingmarson's bawdy house last night when a quarrel broke out. Milly McGhee was shot through the fleshy part of the thigh six inches below the hip joint. Another soiled dove, Flossie Love, was in bed upstairs when a bullet, believed to have been fired either by Milly, or Trooper Albert Grimes, as they struggled for a gun, hit her in the throat. The ball lodged at the base of the tongue and nearly severed it. It was extracted by Dr George Rosen of this city, who also attended to a corporal shot in the shoulder, and a soldier who had a

49

severely splintered shin bone.

The soldier who started the shindig was taken into custody by Marshal Anderson and lodged in the town jail. It is understood Red has taken a vacation for the sake of his health. That might be wise because the cavalry in their camp not far from this city are in a menacing frame of mind.

'They are, are they?' Anderson muttered, as he read the news-sheet in his office. 'Sounds like the sooner we git you up before a judge the better it'll be.'

He passed *The Clarion* through the bars to Grimes, who studied it and cried, 'I'm famous! I got head-lines.'

'Yeah,' Anderson replied, gruffly, as he gave him a tin mug of coffee. 'Lucky you.'

'What about some grub, Marshal?'

'You can sing for it. I got a date with a glass of whiskey over at The Longhorn.'

'What about prisoner's rights?' Grimes wailed. 'I'm starving.'

'You'll have to wait,' Anderson yelled, as he slammed the jailhouse door and locked up. 'I never was fond of bluebellies,' he muttered. He flicked a dime to a passing boy delivering ice. 'Here, son, buy yourself a toffee apple. I'm feelin' generous today.'

There was a brooding sense of malevolence settled over the quiet streets as folks stayed in their houses. If they were expecting trouble it was not long in coming. As dusk fell a contingent of cavalry came trotting into Abilene, forming a circle of mounted men, their carbines at the ready, around the jailhouse.

The moustachioed sergeant swung down and hammered on the locked door with the butt of his revolver. 'Hand over the prisoner,' he shouted. 'Or do you want us to start shootin'?' It was no idle threat. The Seventh, under Custer's command, were renowned for their brutality.

Anderson held his breath for a few seconds, his heart hammering. He poked the barrel of his Creedmore through the bars of an open window and spoke out. 'Come and get him, but you'll have to go past me first.'

'You looking for more bloodshed, Marshal? I advise you you've got no legal right to hold Trooper Grimes. Hand him over: we'll deal with him.'

'Get lost,' Anderson growled, and levered a slug into the Creedmore.

But suddenly he saw the sky behind the town turned to a reddened glow and shrill cries in the distance. 'My boys are burning Red's saloon to the ground,' the sergeant shouted, by way of explanation. 'You want us to set the whole town ablaze, too?'

'You can't do that,' Anderson cried.

'Can't we? You just watch, mister. Which is it going to be?'

'Aw, hail, I can't fight the whole damn US Army,' Anderson muttered. He found his keys and unlocked the cell. 'You're being sprung, pal.' He unlocked the front door and shoved Grimes outside. 'Here he is, the smelly skunk. You can have him. Now call your men off.'

The sergeant leered at him, indicated Grimes to

climb on to a spare bronc, saluted casually and, before leading his column away, shouted, 'Glad you seen sense, Marshal.'

'Yeah, well, good riddance to bad rubbish.' But Anderson felt considerably cowed by events as he clutched his carbine and followed on foot.

The cavalrymen had been incensed to hear that Red had been seen that day catching an express locomotive east towards Kansas City. They had intended to punish him. They had also come armed with cans of kerosene. As the ladies of the night, in their skimpy costumes, ran screaming from the premises, the First or Last Chance was set ablaze.

The troopers watched and cheered as barrels of whiskey and bottles of hooch exploded from within and flames and burning cinders soared into the night sky. 'How's that for high?' one shouted.

Anderson reached the scene in time to see the cavalry forming into a neat column and riding away into the darkness. 'Whoo!' he cried, shielding his eyes. 'Ain't much we can do now.'

When Jane Cox arrived looking for her story, he drawled, 'You gotta look on the bright side, baby. Nobody else got hurt.'

Red Ingmarson was not best pleased to return from a short spell in Kansas City with a bandaged finger stub to find his bordello a pile of smouldering ashes. What was worse, his girls had deserted and were ensconced in Rosy Joe's joint.

'What you whining at, you yeller-livered rat,' Joe roared at him, standing on the stoop of his premises with a loaded shotgun in his hands. 'You ran out on 'em to save your own skin, so they've decided to work for me.'

Red pleaded with the girls to return. 'This my land and I gonna build a new place. You'll get the biggest cut on your earnings in Kansas, *ja*! You don't want to stay with that swindler. Please to come back,' he begged, but the girls, from the safety of their top-storey windows just showered him with insults and laughing obscenities.

'You'll regret this,' Red shouted.

In the next weeks he started feverishly rebuilding his saloon, anxious to get it ready before the cow season began.

As the timber walls were raised he looked out of its unglazed windows with covetous glances at Rosy Joe's place. One afternoon, half-soused in whiskey, he raised his carbine when he saw Joe in his stupid top hat standing at a window. He had him in his sights. Yes, the temptation was too much. Automatically his finger squeezed and Joe's titfer went flying. There were screams from within the premises.

Joe didn't hesitate. He strutted across to Red's building works. As he entered the roofless edifice he shouted, 'You've killed Fast Fingers Annie, you fool! Come on, you crawling snake, face me if you claim to be a man.'

Red jerked up his carbine, but fired too fast, in a panic. Rosy Joe unerringly put both barrels of shot from the twelve gauge in his adversary's chest, bowling him over.

'Aw, not more trouble,' Anderson groaned, roused from a snooze in one of the cells by the shots. 'Better go take a look.'

He saddled his mare and cantered down the trail. Rosy Joe, his plug hat tipped over one eye, was sitting in his rocker on his porch, a shotgun rested on his knees.

Anderson had taken a quick look at Red's bleeding corpse. He stepped down from his horse and eased a slug into his carbine. 'I take it you're responsible for this, Joe?'

'It was self-defence. That madman fired on us. His bullet creased my neck and killed Annie. You'll find her inside. Kate and all the gals will bear witness to what happened. Best of luck, Marshal. You looking to take me in?'

Anderson gave his grim-lipped grin. 'That's what they pay me for, Joe.'

'You sure you wanna earn that miserable pittance?'

Anderson raised the Creedmore. 'Sure I'll earn it.'

Rosy Joe laughed and tossed his shotgun down into the dust. 'If you're offering me the hospitality of your hoosegow, I accept. No doubt you'll allow me to pay to have some decent food brought in?' He dug in the inside pocket of his frock coat and produced a wallet. He flicked a finger through a wad of greenbacks. 'Y'all see I got nine hundred dollars here. Questions will be asked of the marshal if it ain't intact when he releases me. In the meantime you keep the place going, gals. This here's your wages. And there'll be a bonus for y'all and one hell of a party when I come out. I might even sue the marshal for wrongful arrest.'

'Shee-it!' Anderson whistled through his teeth, as he put the cuffs on Joe. 'Why did I take this cruddy job?'

He whistled to the mare to follow along and escorted Joe back to the jailhouse. 'Everything's taken care of,' he told Clarence Hooson, who came running from his bank. 'You better send for the judge. Joe here will stand trial for killin' Red after the Norwegian killed one of his dancin' gals.'

When the mayor had been briefed and Joe lodged in a cell, Anderson got hold of a horse and wagon to go collect the corpses of Red and poor Annie. He dragged them into the coroner's morgue, searched them and listed their possessions. Annie had a pouch of silver dollars in her calico drawers.

'Those are the last fast bucks Annie'll make,' he drawled, as he returned to the jailhouse and tossed them on his desk, along with about $300 from Red's pockets.

'How about joining me for dinner, Marshal?' Rosy Joe was sitting in his cell, puffing at a cigar. He took a twenty from his overstuffed wallet and passed it through the bars. 'Order for two over at The Longhorn with a bottle of California wine.'

'Who d'you think I am, your damn lackey?' Anderson hesitated, angrily. Then accepted the bill. 'OK. Give me the wallet and whatever else you got. I'll put it in the safe.'

'There's nine hundred dollars in there. You look

after me, my young friend, and I'll look after you.'

Anderson gave him a scoffing grin. 'Sure.' He counted the wad of notes. 'Nine hundred and fifty-five to be precise. I'd better put that in my report.'

'No need to bother, Marshal. I'll be spending a tidy bit if I'm gonna be your guest.' Joe winked. 'You get my drift.'

'You trying to bribe me, mister?'

'Sure. A hundred of that would help oil the wheels of justice, wouldn't it?'

'Yeah, maybe it would. But not with me. I'm going ahead with this trial.'

The marshal found a form, pen and ink and began to write. 'Full name?'

'Joseph Rose.'

'Just tell me in your own words what happened.' He was no great pen-man and struggled to scratch it down. 'Not so fast.' When it was done, he took it across. 'Sign here.'

'Now I need you to find me an attorney.'

'First things first. What you fancy? T-bone steak and fries?'

'Yeah, and bring a bottle of gin, too. Might as well make myself comfortable, eh, Marshal?'

As he strolled over to The Longhorn, Jane Cox came from her office and crossed over to him, taking tiny, hurried strides in her tight, ankle-length skirt. 'Marshal!'

'Come inside. I'll buy you a drink and give you the lowdown.'

'I don't think I should. Well, a sarsparilla.'

He beckoned her into a booth, squeezing in beside her. 'You with the Ladies Temperance League?'

Jane flicked through her notebook, a trifle disconcerted as Anderson put his arm along the back of the seat, his grey eyes studying her. 'Can I have the facts? Have you charged him?'

'Yep, second degree homicide. He's elected trial.'

When Jim arrived with their drinks the marshal drawled, twirling the twenty dollar bill, 'I'd like steaks for two an' the trimmings, bottle of California, one of gin. Take it over to the jailhouse.'

Jane raised an eyebrow. 'Rosy Joe seems to be living rather well. I assume that's his twenty?'

'True. If he wants to pay for my supper an' his own, an' split a bottle I ain't objecting. It's saving the city taxpayers' money.'

'To me that sounds like bribery.'

'A steak and drink ain't gonna buy Joe any favours. As a matter of interest he offered me a hundred but I turned him down. Same goes for Red. He wanted me to *represent* him for fifty a week.'

'Is that why you didn't bring charges against Red for shooting those two troopers?'

'No, it ain't,' Anderson replied, angrily. 'I ain't been bought. I was tempted, I admit. But not yet. If you really wanna know, I didn't want him moaning and wailing all night in my jailhouse about his missing finger. I like to get some sleep.'

Jane suddenly froze as the marshal's right hand squeezed her thigh beneath the table. She was jammed up against the wall in the booth and felt trapped. She picked up his hand with icy fingers and replaced it on the table. 'Please, Marshal, do you mind? I'm not one of your dance-hall girls.'

'Nope.' He coiled a strand of her hair with the forefinger of his left hand and stared at her intently. 'You gotta bear with me, Jane. I'm new at this game. The mayor told me to be nice to the Press.'

She shook his hand away, indignantly. 'I don't think he meant like this.'

'Why don't you join me over in my jailhouse one night? It gets mighty lonesome.'

'No thank you,' she replied, icily. 'I don't know what's given you these ideas but I can assure you I am not remotely interested in a man who guzzles whiskey, who smokes – a most noxious habit – and who seems ready to shoot first and ask questions later.'

'You want me to give up whiskey and cigars and start going to church? I wouldn't be the same man.'

Jane turned and met his, eyes. 'It's my impression you had a bad start in life, Mr Anderson. Maybe, if a river's started on a certain course it is impossible to change. If you gave me an indication that you want to settle down, lead a decent life, then maybe—'

Anderson grinned widely. 'I'm putty in your hands, Jane. Let's see – how about joining me for a gallop in the morning? I gotta exercise my grey. We could talk.'

'Perhaps,' she said, making a move to get out of the booth. 'If that's all you plan to exercise.'

SIX

The Longhorn was packed for the trial of Rosy Joe. The judge, Herbert van Trees, in a starched collar and suit, perched on a high stool behind the bar, peered over his wire spectacles, and banged his gavel for order.

'If there are any more interruptions,' he fluted in his reedy voice, 'I'll have the courtroom cleared.'

Joe, or Joseph Rose as he was named in the charge, sprawled indolently in his chair, attired in frock coat, cravat with a diamond stickpin, and fancy waistcoat, his attorney, Mr Tommy Tucker, by his side.

'Good for you, Judge,' the brothel-keeper growled. 'Let's get on with it, shall we?'

The audience was divided between the respectables on one side and the less respectable denizens of the town's saloons, cowhands, drunks, drifters and railroadmen, there out of curiosity, ready with ripe comments and lusty laughter as Marshal Anderson tried to get some sense out of the string of witnesses.

Mainly, these were bawds from Joe's troupe, led by

Big Kate, perfumed and painted, in a huge flowered hat and rustling silks, her Chihuahua in her arms as she took the stand.

Asked her profession, Kate drawled,'An entertainer, you could say.' And her marital status? 'I guess I'm Mr Rose's concubine.'

An old galoot in the front row, puffing his pipe, cackled, 'What's that? A fancy word for his whore? Go on, show us a leg, Kate. Give us a song!'

The jury, all male, of course, sat along one side, a mixture of shopkeepers and small farmers from the outlying district. 'How much longer we got to be here?' one protested. 'I got my chooks to feed. Lot of prairie foxes about. Need to lock 'em up 'fore dusk.'

'I guess I'm done, if the defence is,' the marshal drawled. 'The fact is, much as Joe mighta been riled up, he had no right to take the law into his own hands. He shoulda sent for me.'

The judge mopped his brow with a kerchief. 'In that case I will ask the jury to withdraw and consider their verdict.'

Joe called out, 'I'd like to buy each of 'em a drink 'fore they go. You, too, Judge.'

'Denied,' van Trees cried. 'Quite out of the question.'

'Aw, come on, yer honour,' the foreman of the jury moaned. 'We could see thangs in more perspective with a whiskey in our bellies.'

'Oh, very well, if it will hurry things up.' Van Trees raised a finger to the barkeep. 'Jim, one drink each. Make mine a brandy. I've got a train to catch, so make it quick, boys.'

'Outrageous!' a church-going lady shrieked. 'This is blatant bribery.'

'Aw, shut up, you old bat,' one of the jury called. 'It ain't often we git anything outa Rosy Nose Joe.'

'It's a travesty of justice,' Jane Cox said, when the marshal went over to chat to her while they awaited the jury. 'I intend to say so in my editorial.'

Anderson shrugged. 'You gotta give some leeway, Jane. Folks got their own way of doing things in the West.'

'Not guilty,' was the verdict, greeted with raucous cheers on one side and hisses of disapproval by the other.

'Hang on,' the marshal shouted. 'I ain't done yet. There's another charge. The state of Kansas versus Joseph Rose.' He had reluctantly been persuaded by the town committee to bring this one and, not being a good reader, droned out the charge, '. . . that on the fifteenth day of May the aforesaid did set up and maintain a common bawdy house and brothel for the succour and gain of the said Joseph Rose and women of evil name and fame and of dishonest conversation, at unlawful times at night as well as day, and unlawfully did permit the corruption of good morals, being a common nuisance to all the citizens of the state residing in the neighbourhood. How about that, Joe?'

'Not guilty,' Joe said. 'All I run in my house is Bible school for unfortunate gals. They'll tell you that.'

Judge van Trees consulted his lawbooks. 'I fail to see how a town bylaw can be applied to an establishment beyond its jurisdiction. You've hanged yourselves by your own petard, citizens. Case dismissed. This court session is now closed.'

As a gang of rowdies grabbed Joe and hoisted him shoulder high, Anderson looked at Jane and shrugged. 'That's the way it goes. Fancy a stroll along to The Bull?'

'No, I don't.' She picked up her notebook and papers with a flourish. 'I've got a story to write.'

The brim of her purple felt hat, with its peacock feather, was bent back by the force of the wind as Jane Cox galloped her chestnut across the prairie, urging it faster in an effort to catch up with Anderson who was charging on ahead, the steel-clad hoofs of his grey kicking up shards of turf. He was a fine horseman – she would give him that – riding poised as an Indian, almost part of the horse. He pulled in and waited for her on the crest of one of the rolling, green grass mounds, and Jane laughed, out-of-breath, as she joined him.

'I guess you won,' she gasped.

'She needs plenty of exercise,' Anderson replied, slapping the mare's neck. 'Gotta keep her in trim. In fact, I been thinkin' of entering her in the long distance event at the town races this summer. Hear the prize money's pretty good.'

'Of course, you had the advantage of me,' Jane smiled, as she adjusted her bright hat, and smoothed the billowing riding skirt. 'Riding side-saddle isn't designed for speed.'

'Waal,' he grinned, turning the mare, 'you can allus cock your leg *over* while you're out here. Nobody ain't gonna see, except me, of course.'

Jane's smile faded. There was sometimes an uncouth suggestiveness to the marshal's comments. His quiet demeanour belied the dangerous currents that ran beneath. Maybe it had been reckless of her to accept his invitation, offered in his mocking way, to join her for a morning ride, if not downright foolish, it occurred to her, now that they were alone and miles from anywhere. Jane had been confident she could keep the marshal at a distance, but now, as he looked at her, she was not so sure.

'Waal, what do you want to do?' he drawled. 'Lie down in the grass while we give the hosses a rest?'

'I'd rather not,' she said. 'I've got a lot to do. We can jog them back. But I'm glad I came. It's blown away the cobwebs after sitting in that so-called court-room for two days.'

'Yeah, I see you're campaigning to have a proper courthouse raised.'

In her article Jane had bemoaned the fact that the case had been 'conducted in such hopeless surround-ings, a bar room in which Rosy Joe, to give him his inelegant cognomen, had seemed most at ease.'

She had also laid into his witnesses – a succession of frail females in whom any sense of modesty and right has long since been sacrificed with their virtue on the altar of sin and who obviously cared not a fig for the obligations of the oath.

Jane had told her father she wanted to get closer to

Anderson to find out just what were the dark secrets of his past he hinted at. But, if she were honest, it might be true that his air of recklessness disturbed and, in some strange way, attracted her.

She watched him as he rode, jerked out his carbine, and from the saddle shot a plump prairie chicken that had jumped up from the grass with a clatter of wings. He rode back to lean down and scoop it up. 'Tomorrow's supper,' he said. 'Tonight I'm gonna treat myself and sample the menu at The Alamo. Fancy joining me?'

'I don't know.' She hesitated, unable to deny that the lanky marshal made her heart thump when he looked at her like that. 'Quite frankly, Mr Anderson, I don't care for your roving hands. You're too fresh.'

'OK, Jane, I'll be on my best behaviour. It's your mind that stimulates me, anyway. You could bring your notebook, pretend you're interviewing me if you're worried about what your churchy friends might think.'

'Small-town gossip, you mean,' she remarked, as they rode the mares back across the vast tract of prairie until Abilene came in sight. 'Well, I have to protect my reputation.'

'Yeah,' he muttered. 'I guess you have.'

He rubbed the mare down and went back into the jail-house to catch up with some paperwork. He had been unable to discover any next of kin for Red or Fast Fingers Annie. Their cash would go into town funds. 'Might just as well have put it in my own pocket,' he reflected, as he filled in the form on Ingmarson.

'Cause of death: shotgunned.' It had begun to annoy him that he had found little extra income to his salary as yet. 'My ranch fund ain't growin' none.'

He tossed his pen down with disgust and stepped outside to get some air. He stood on the sidewalk, his thumbs hitched in his gunbelt, and watched the comings and goings on the wide, dusty main drag. Although out of season it was busy enough. A farmer was loading sacks of flour on to his wagon outside Smith and Ross's grocery store. Two gentlemen of colour who not long before would no doubt have been Southern slaves – there had been 115,000 of them in Missouri – were driving a double-wagon bull train out of town, hauled by eight yoke of oxen and loaded with supplies to sell in far-flung settlements not reached by the railroad. At the same time, a couple of bedraggled buffalo skinners, in their filthy buckskins, were hauling a big bison on a travois behind their horses into the meat market. All the various booze joints along the strip were doing sporadic trade. A couple of children were playing with hoops in the street as other riders clipped by. A one-legged veteran of the war, Jim Goodwin, was blowing his harmonica, a tin can ready for coins. And a family – man, woman, and kids – were manhandling from one of the flatbed trucks lined up on the rail, a prefabricated house chosen from a Chicago mail order catalogue.

The fellow was scratching his head, saying, 'I cain't make much sense of this. It's gonna take some assembling.' Anderson jumped down to help load the wooden struts and triangles on to his wagon. 'Aw, you'll manage,' he said.

Bee-keepers, barbers, bootmakers, the cigar store and billiards hall were all doing steady business. In other words, Abilene was quietly seething with the energetic striving of settlers on the frontier to make an honest buck.

'So, how many men have you killed?' Jane Cox asked, as they sat in the dining room of The Alamo.

Anderson was in the middle of carving into a thick and juicy buffalo steak. He had pulled a razor-sharp scalping knife from a fringed and beaded sheath hanging from his gunbelt as the knives provided by the saloon and gaming house were kind of puny. He paused, knife in hand. 'What kind of question is that?'

Jane had chosen a more easily managed chicken salad and sat with notebook open by her side. 'It was your idea I interview you.'

'In times of war you don't have time to keep count of the casualties, ya just keep on shooting.'

'What regiment were you with?'

Anderson chewed on the steak before he answered. 'It weren't exactly a regiment. We were irregulars.'

'Did you volunteer?'

'Nope. I was what sailors call shanghaied at the age of fifteen.' He munched some more. 'It ain't something I wanna talk about. Bad things happen in a civil war. Innocent civilians in the line of fire, they're the ones who git hurt.'

'OK, we'll skip the war. How about since then? How many men you gunned down?'

66

Anderson spooned cranberry sauce over his meat. 'Let's say most of the varmints asked for it, or it was them or me.'

When he had called for Jane at the cottage she and her father rented, she had been ready and waiting in a satin dress of emerald-green stripes, pinned at the throat by a cameo. Her father had not looked too pleased, grunting a greeting, but she had put on her purple hat and a Mexican shawl and trotted along beside him to the restaurant, a room set aside from the gaming area. There were only a couple of other tables taken and conversation was restrained.

'People say the way you stopped Bloody Bob in his tracks with that shot to his arm was remarkable,' Jane persisted. 'Would you call yourself a fast gun?'

'No, that was a pure fluke. I was trying to kill him,' he replied, with a grin, so she couldn't tell if he was joking or not. 'Still, it don't do no harm to let folks think I'm fast. It might put some off trying me. Let's see, shall we try some oysters? Escalloped, whatever that is?'

'Why not?' she laughed. 'It's not every day I indulge.'

'You mean there ain't no money in the newspaper game?'

'Very little. That's why we've gone tri-weekly, to increase our income. Dad's been toying with the idea of putting a picture on the front page, but it's not financially viable at the moment.'

'So why do you do it?'

'He's got the newspaperman bug. He couldn't do anything else. He has a bad heart, so since my mother

67

died I've felt honour bound to look after him.'

Anderson tipped the first of half-a-dozen oysters down his throat from its shell and met her sparkling grey eyes as she did the same. 'Pretty good, huh? They say these thangs stimulate a man's certain parts.'

Jane made a down-turned grimace. 'In that case you'd better not eat any more.' She tried to turn the conversation back to him. 'So, you've been down in New Mexico?'

'I been a lot of places.' He showed her his razor-sharp knife with the bone handle carved as a coyote's head. 'This is a souvenir from there. An Apache tried to jump me in a ravine west of Silver City. He was after my scalp. Luckily I came off best an' kept my hair.'

'Eugh!' Jane said. 'I presume what you're saying is you've led a pretty wild life. My father's convinced you have something to hide.'

Anderson tipped another oyster down his throat. 'That's for him to guess and me to know.' He returned the knife to its sheath. 'How about you, Jane? You had many men in your life? You done anything you're ashamed of?'

Jane snapped the notebook shut. 'OK, let's forget the interview. If you're implying that I'm pining for some lost love, or that, at my age, I'm desperate not to become an old maid, you're barking up the wrong tree, Marshal. Impertinently, too.'

Anderson laughed and let go her hand. 'That's what I like about you. All the gals I've met heretofore have been real bird brains, thinkin' only of fashions, cooking, sewing, hooking a man and popping out umpteen brats.'

'A noble vocation.'

'Yeah, but you're different. You got a real head on your shoulders.'

As they finished their oysters, the casino owner, Vern Atkinson, a suave character in a grey suit with lilac piping to match his frilled shirt, came over. 'Good to see you, Marshal, and you, Miss Cox. Going to play the tables?'

'Why not? But first I'd like some of your apple pie? How about you, sweetheart?'

Jane looked taken aback by the word, but studied the menu. 'Blancmange and ice cream would be nice.'

The marshal ran fingers through his thick, wavy hair that curled back over the collar of his blue shirt, and stuck his boots out while they waited. 'It's a dangerous game running a newspaper, ain't it? I've heard of editors being tarred and feathered, their presses smashed, even killed by men they've maligned in their columns.'

'Some men can't take the truth,' she replied. 'So perhaps I should tell *you* the truth and that is that the reason I accepted this invitation is that I would like to know the truth about you. If I'm to take a man seriously I would like him not to lie, or use subterfuge.'

'You don't say?' That silenced the marshal for a bit and he concentrated on his apple pie. Then he pulled out a cheroot and asked, 'Mind if I smoke?'

'If you must.'

'Yes, I must.' He lit up and asked, 'Why'd you wear your hair pulled back like a schoolmarm all the time? Why not let it down? It'd suit you.'

'Thank you for the fashion tip, Marshal. I'll bear it in mind.'

'You're too sharp, Jane. I don't mean no harm.' He got to his feet. 'C'mon, let's take a look. Or you got somethang aginst gamblin', too?'

'Whiskey and cards are the cause of most of the trouble in this town.'

'Don't I know it! It's been the ruination of many a man. But don't worry, I can't afford to go mad. Just to show you I ain't no gambler, I'll risk twenty dollars, that's all.'

Jane was studying the large oil painting over the bar of a Rubensesque, sparsely draped nude. 'I guess that's the cowboy's idea of heaven.'

'Yep.' He asked for a Kentucky bourbon and an iced lemonade for her and led her across to the roulette wheel. Out of season the tables were not crowded, just a quiet, studied activity in the flickering light of a candelabra. He bought a handful of chips and placed a couple of dollars worth on the marked board, watched the wheel spin, the ivory ball go clicketing around. 'I ain't a dab hand at this game.'

To the marshal's suprise he started to win. 'Here, you try. You're bringing me luck.'

'What do I do?' Jane asked, as the croupier called, 'Place your bets, folks.'

'Any number you like.'

Against her better instincts, the young woman began to get excited as their winnings mounted. She started brandishing her fist, urging the wheel to do the same again. 'Yes!' she cried.

Anderson glanced aside and noticed Atkinson give a nod to the croupier. He was letting them win. The wheel game was fixed. 'Come on. Let's go while we're twenty dollars up, afore you get addicted.'

He cashed the chips, paid the bill, and wrapped her shawl around her shoulders, stepping out into the early summer's night. A couple of coyotes had sneaked into town to poke at the rubbish piles, but ran off at their approach. 'Town's quiet,' he said.'I guess it's the lull before the storm.'

'Yes, the herds will be here soon. Then you'll have to earn your spurs, Marshal.'

'Fancy coming in the jailhouse for a nice cup of coffee?' he asked.

'No, I think not,' she murmured. 'You've had enough luck for tonight, Hank.'

'Well, you never know. Maybe another night.'

'I'll think about it.'

When they reached the door of the cottage he caught hold of her by her slim waist and pulled her into him, dipping his head to kiss her lips. But Jane turned her face away and the kiss brushed her cheek.

'Goodnight, Hank,' she said, extricating herself. 'It's been an interesting day.'

'Hey,' he called, as she turned away. 'haven't you forgotten something?'

'What?'

'Your share of the winnings.' He pressed a ten-dollar bill into her hand. 'You better not tell Daddy how you earned it.'

SEVEN

Quiet Abilene was not, for long. Anderson had an urgent summons early the next morning from Jim, the barkeep, complaining that a crazy Indian, Spotted Horse, had come into his back kitchen demanding to be given breakfast. 'I gave him a darned good feast, a sackful of bread and cold meat to get rid of him,' he wailed. 'But then he started abusing poor old Sal who washes our pots and says he ain't gonna leave.'

Spotted Horse had made his way up from the Nations on a two-horse wagon and set up camp on a spare lot on Texas Street. Then, in the words of *The Clarion* the next day: *The Pawnee began to barter the person of his squaw to the lusts of two-legged white animals in whom the dog instinct prevails.*

Hank buckled on his gunbelt and went outside to take a look. Spotted Horse, he was told, had wandered off up the street, waving his knife and scaring the daylights out of any passer-by he met.

A boy came running to announce that the half-naked Pawnee was now in The Alamo causing mayhem and could the marshal come quick. 'Looks like I'm gonna have to earn them roulette winnings,' he muttered, 'don't it?'

Spotted Horse was wearing little more than a loin-cloth, leggings, moccasins, a whiteman's waistcoat, wampum around his throat, and a Lincoln hat deco-rated with feathers, under which hung his black plaits. He was standing unsteadily at the bar, roaring and stamping like a rutting buffalo.

On the far side, Vern Atkinson was fending him off with a broom. His pallor gave him the look of a proverbial paleface. 'He's demanding whiskey,' he screamed. 'When I said it ain't allowed he started hurl-ing glasses at me. Look at all the damage he's done.'

When he saw the marshal the Pawnee gave an ugly grimace and hurled one at him, too.

'Hold it right there, man,' Anderson shouted. 'You go git on your wagon and git outa this town right now.'

'Maybe you should send for Mr Covington, the interpreter,' the casino boss suggested.

At that, Spotted Horse came out with a volley of obscene abuse in Anglo-Saxon telling them just where they could go. 'Gimme whiskey, you sonsabitches,' he roared.

'I don't believe he needs one,' Anderson said, step-ping up close to get hold of the Pawnee's arm. 'There's only one language this gentleman under-stands. Come on, pal, you've had your fun.'

The burly Indian suddenly brought up his knife with his free hand and swung it hard at Anderson's face. The marshal ducked, there was a violent struggle and he looked to be getting the worst of it as he was pinned back down against the bar. Inbred years of instinct made him slip out his own Apache scalper and, as he held Spotted Horse back, he thrust upwards stuck it hard in his chest, twisted it, and stuck him again.

'I didn't want to kill him,' he told Jane later after the Pawnee had expired, lying on the floor of the saloon in a pool of his own blood. 'That's the way it goes.'

'Look at the mess he's made,' Vern Atkinson moaned, coming out from behind the bar with his broom and starting to clear up. 'You did what you had to, Marshal. The next time you two are in here it will be on the house.'

Jane gave him a quizzical look. 'What about his wife?'

'She ain't waited to pick up his body,' Jim announced. 'When she heard the news she jumped on the wagon and whipped them hosses outa here fast as she could go. She's headed back towards the Nations in a cloud of dust.'

KILLED BY THE MARSHAL was the headline in the next morning's *Clarion*, with a full account of the affair, concluding: *Coroner Stevenson viewed the body last night, held an inquest and the jury reached the verdict that the deceased came to his death from wounds inflicted by a knife in the hand of Marshal Henry Anderson and that this was done in the discharge of his duties as an officer of the law in protection of lives and property of this community.*

Fear of Indian raids was ever present on the frontier

as for two years past war parties of Cheyenne had been attacking outlying homesteads, killing, burning and raping. So nobody was likely to condemn the marshal for ending the life of one fool Pawnee. In fact, most congratulated him. Few entertained the thought that the tribes might have legitimate grievances. That they had been robbed of their livelihood as millions of bison were slaughtered for their hides on the southern plains, the carcasses left to rot, did not seem to bother whites who cared mostly for their own safety.

Meanwhile, it was rumoured that the Cheyenne had drifted north of the Platte and the cross-continent railroad to join their brother Sioux on the northern prairies where there were still herds of buffalo and game to sustain them. There were, it was claimed, some 20,000 Indians gathered there and they were in a warlike mood, vowing to make a last stand against white invasion of their lands.

That they might have good reason to feel agitated was evident from another item in the same issue of *The Clarion*: *Grand Duke Alexis of Russia, with a party numbering 500, including four companies of US cavalry and regimental band, led by General Sheridan and Lt.Col. George Custer, no less, was engaged in a hunting expedition along the North Platte. A single day's tally was 200 buffalo and,* Editor Cox commented, *they are busily engaged in exterminating most of the wildlife in the area.*

A lawman's life was not all trouble and strife. Hank had started driving Jane in her buggy to church of a Sunday morning, tipping his hat to the settlers' wives in their best bonnets. It was as much a social gathering as an occasion of worship, although the black-bearded preacher, the Revd. Copsey, blasted the fear of God into them from his pulpit. Anderson sat in one of the front pews, propping his Creedmore by him, alongside the doctor, lawyer, land agent and leading citizens. He barely believed a word of what the preacher was booming on about, apart from the 'eye for an eye' Old Testament parts. But just being there made him, too, a pillar of the community.

'Just how hypocritical can you get?' he muttered to himself as he set the surrey moving with a flick of the whip afterwards. He had been invited to a roast dinner and he was in a hurry to get back to the cottage.

'What do you mean?' Jane asked, sharply.

'I mean me, kneelin' in that pew chanting my amens along with y'all. *Thou shalt not kill.* Heck, you people pay me to do your killin' for ya.'

Jane pursed her lips, making no comment until her father had said grace and was carving the prairie turkey. 'Hank tells me he's an atheist and doesn't believe in thanking the Lord for his bounty.'

'What?' the white-haired Aaron Cox cried, brandishing the carving knife. 'Don't tell me you agree with that fellow Darwin that we're all descended from monkeys? Mind you, in view of the hooligans we see around here he might have a point. Can you eat a leg, young man?'

'I guess I could try.' Anderson grinned as his plate was piled high. 'I don't mean to disrespect your beliefs. I just don't share 'em. It's you and Jane I would thank for the bounty of this fine meal.'

'You shot the turkey, but I believe God provided him.' Jane smiled as she pushed across a steaming bowl. 'Have some sweet potatoes, Marshal. You need to keep up your strength.'

As they sat under the shade of a cottonwood tree in the garden afterwards, Aaron Cox commented, 'You know, Hank, not many intelligent men believe *everything* in the Bible these days. To me religion is more of a moral philosophy, the way a man lives his life.'

'And a woman, too.' Jane got to her feet. 'I know I shouldn't work on a Sunday but I've got tomorrow's edition to put to bed.'

'How about me putting *you* to bed?' Anderson suggested, when they were alone. But Jane avoided his embrace. 'I'm not ready for that, Hank. I'm not sure about you. I don't really know you, do I?'

'No,' Anderson muttered. 'I guess you don't.'

The young reporter was friendly and vivacious, but a strict believer. As time passed Anderson sensed a seething sexuality within her angular but attractive body. If so, she was in no hurry to bare it to him, always deflecting his embraces. 'It's gonna be a long, hard courtship,' he warned himself. Did he want to go the whole hog? he wondered. Wasn't it just a case of trying to get his hands on what he couldn't get? Was he ready to get hogtied in the marriage bonds, even if she would *have* him? Overweening respect for a woman was a dangerous thing.

'I seen too many American husbands willingly led by their wimmin like tame bears with rings through their snouts,' he told the barkeep Jim one day. 'I ain't aiming to be like them. I ain't ready to be tamed just yet.'

The summer was still young, the glorious green of the prairie yet to turn dry and sere as the sun beat down. There were several jolly church outings and an annual picnic along the river. Although there was little danger, the marshal was asked to ride along with his guns to provide protection. It was a pleasant day, the children shrilly playing, the adults chattering and preparing the barbecue and treats.

'Hiya, Lizzie,' Hank called, as he saw the saddler's daughter sitting alone on the river-bank. 'A penny for your thoughts.'

'I was thinking of you, Mr Anderson.' The girl smiled up at him coyly. 'Of how handsome you look on your horse.'

The marshal glanced around but nobody seemed to be taking any notice of him, so he sat down in the long grass beside her. 'Maybe I'll give you a ride one of these days,' he said, with a smile.

Lizzie stretched out in her rustling summer dress, her blue eyes gazing into his, stroking back a strand of her blonde hair, thick and bright as ripe corn. 'Mm, that would be nice,' she murmured. Her knee touched his as she turned towards him and her slim fingers reached out to his thigh. Suddenly the marshal was kissing her sweet, cherubic lips. He could not resist.

'Mr Anderson!' Lizzie exclaimed, sitting up, straightening her dress. 'Really, I never thought—'

'Hank's the handle.' His heart was not the only part of his anatomy that was pounding. 'You tryin' to tease me, Lizzie?'

'No-oh,' she cooed, tying the ribbons of her straw sunhat. She gave him a cheeky smile. 'Shall we go for a stroll along the bank? It looks nice an' shady under them trees.'

'I dunno.' Hank tried to put his mind on other things. She's only fifteen, he warned himself. This is crazy. He stood and looked back at the picnic folks. Nobody was watching them. Why should they? He put out a hand to help the girl to her feet. 'What the hell,' he said. 'Why not?'

'Has anybody seen my daughter?' the saddler, Jim Upstone, asked some while later.

'Why *there* she is!' A woman pointed along the bank. The tall figure of Anderson was coming out of the trees, the girl hanging on to his arm. 'She's been walking with the marshal.'

'If that's what you call it,' a man muttered.

Anderson tried to look casual as he strolled back to the group, who were staring silently at him and the girl. 'You folks ready to go?' he called.

Then he saw that Jane Cox had come clipping in on her surrey and, as the horse halted, sat with the reins in her hands, staring and, like the others, condemning him, too.

'Aw, shee-it!' he hissed. 'I think we're in trouble.'

Jo de Merritt, a hard-bitten but well-preserved lady of the twilight world, had arrived in Abilene claiming to be Red Ingmarson's former mistress and partner, and flourishing the deeds of land rights to his now half-built saloon. It was rumoured that she had been run out of Newton, a town on the new railroad further south-west, which was vying to cash in on the cattle boom, for her immoral activities. But the land registry rubber-stamped her claim, and Jo set up in business.

'I'm gonna put a roof on the place, build a dozen small bedrooms, and import a real mahogany bar and fittings from back East,' she told the marshal when she called in his office to introduce herself. 'It's going to be the rootin'-est, tootin'-est dance house in the West.'

'So, why you telling me?' Anderson asked.

'Because I'm short of capital.' Jo was sitting in a tight-waisted suit of silver-grey velvet. A hat, with a grey felt dove, perched atop her silver hair. 'I want to give you the chance to invest. You put in five hundred and I guarantee you'll reap twenty times that by the end of the season. We'll be fifty-fifty partners.'

'Why me?'

With her scarlet fingernails Miss de Merritt fitted a tailored cigarette into a slim silver holder and eyed him, astutely. 'Because I'm scared of Rosy Joe. He won't like the competition. And when Rosy don't like something he turns ugly. I wouldn't put it past him hiring some bully boys to smash up the place, and me, too, putting me in the hospital and outa business.'

'Yeah?' Hank put one boot toe up on his desk and rocked back and forth in his swivel chair. 'Waal, I ain't worried about him.'

'Good.' Jo, a lady of uncertain age, daggered out

smoke from her nostrils. 'So, you're interested?'

Anderson stroked his unruly hair from his eyes, reached in his drawer and brought out a bottle of Kentucky bourbon. 'Five hundred, huh? So happens I've got that much.' He jerked out the stopper and poured two half-tumblers, pushing one across his desk to her. 'It's a gamble, ain't it?'

'No, it's a certainty. I got the contacts, the girls. I know the game. You can't lose. Fifty per cent of the receipts each week. You don't need to say you're involved. Be the silent partner. You have the right as a lawman to protect me from Rosy Joe. That's all I ask of you.'

'You ain't asking much.' Anderson drawled the sarcasm after taking a bite of the bourbon. 'I ain't easy about this. It could end in disaster. For all of us. Rosy Joe, like you say, plays dirty.'

'Come on, Marshal,' de Merritt sneered. 'Where's your guts? Your take could be as high as two-fifty a week. What you got to lose? This crummy job?'

'Huh!' Anderson gave a gasp of contempt. 'Maybe I'd rather be on eighty a month and stay alive.'

'Make your mind up.' Jo tossed back the shot with a grimace of her painted lips. 'Look.' She opened the bag she was hugging to her lacy bosom, picked out a roll of greenbacks, flicked through them. 'This is my five hundred. Half-shares I said. I may be an ex-whore, but I ain't gonna cheat ya. My word's my word.'

'What would you expect? I obviously can't spend all of my time in that joint. What you gonna call it?'

'Jo's Place.'

'I got my other duties, this town to patrol.'

'I'd just need you to call in, maybe mornings, late at nights, be there as and when there's trouble. Stand up to Rosy Joe.'

'Yeah?' Anderson scratched his jaw. Then he unlocked his strongbox, counted out $500 in paper and gold coin, spread it on the desk and pushed it across. 'OK. I'm in. It's all I got.'

'Good.' Jo jumped to her feet with alacrity and stepped forward to embrace him, kissing him on both cheeks. She offered her gloved hand to shake. 'Welcome, partner.' Her green eyes gleamed catlike beneath arched brows. 'You handsome hunk,' she purred. 'You sure make a woman wish she was thirty years younger.'

Jo scooped the cash into her bag, tipped a drop more bourbon into the glass and one for him. 'Here's to us,' she said, raising hers. 'I'll be in touch.'

'Yeah,' he drawled, as she headed for the door. He sipped the bourbon, thoughtfully, a sinking feeling in his stomach, as he watched her through the bars of the window, sashay away, twirling her parasol, up the street in the direction of the railroad station. 'A fool an' his money . . . she'll probably be on the next train outa here.'

EIGHT

The sudden arrival of the first herd hit Abilene like a tidal wave. 'They're coming!' a man shouted, galloping his pinto into town. The citizens ran out of their shops and houses to gape at a great pillar of dust swirling into the sky on the southern horizon. Closer and closer it came. And then 3,000 bawling, horn-clattering beeves were being whipped and yipped into the extensive pens to await loading on to rail vans and shipment to their fate in the slaughter houses of New York and Chicago.

But once that was done the real trouble began. The Texan cowboys in their tall Stetsons and fancy spurs were paid off. They had hundreds of dollars in their pockets and were in a mood to celebrate. They had driven their herd nearly a thousand miles from south of San Antonio, urging them north through the vast Lone Star state, fording the Red River, battling through quick-sands, flash floods, hailstorms, alert to the possible calamity of a stampede, facing hostile Kiowas and Cheyenne in Indian Teritory, urging the line of beasts on and on for nearly three months, crossing the Washita, the Canadian and the Arkansas rivers until they reached the Kansas border and followed a trail marked by buffalo skulls north across the prairie to Abilene.

So, celebrate they did. And how! In the next few days two more herds were driven in hot on their tails. . . .

In the words of Aaron Cox in his editorial: *The town is awash once again with swaggering Texans dead set on wreaking havoc here. Beer and whiskey has been sold without stint. Gambling goes on night and day, from five cent chuck-a-luck to a $1000 poker pot. Ten dance halls have been going full blast where hordes of fast women lurk seeking soft saps. In short, a general hurrah of a time has ensued. Citizens have been kept from sleep by screams, curses and gunshots throughout the night. We wait to see whether our new marshal, Henry Anderson, can face up to this bunch.*

One of the busiest joints was the first one the rip-snorting, free-spending cowhands got to, the newly named Jo's Place. Anderson was often on the stoop to greet them, ordering them to hang their gunbelts on the hooks in the lobby. 'There's gals and booze galore, boys,' he shouted, 'but we don't want no shootin'.'

Standing behind the bar in her grey velvet dress, her silver hair coiffed, Jo de Merritt, too, had the look of a lady who didn't mince her words. A four-piece band, guitar, fiddle, squeezebox and trumpet, was on the bandstand blaring out fast tempo melodies. Her new bar was stocked with whiskey, gin, rum and beer, and three barmen were kept busy serving non-stop as the Texans shouted and shoved through the throng. Her bedrooms alongside one wall were mere plank cubicles, their curtains ready to be swished aside. Jo had met trains from the East and recruited a bevy of wenches who were willing to sell their body and soul for a silver dollar. Miss de Merritt had done her job indecently well.

One night the middle-aged madam had taken a break from raking in the cash and issuing tokens for 'dances' with the girls. 'It's like taking candy from babies,' she grinned, as she slid a glass of clear alcoholic liquid towards Anderson.

'What's this?' he asked.

'Railroad gin. My own brew.'

'I'll pass.' He pushed it back. 'Gimme a beer.'

'I told ya we couldn't lose,' she said, wiping a sheen of sweat from her brow. 'Come by in the morning and I'll tell you how much we've made.'

It was inevitable there would be trouble. It flared up on this occasion after midnight among a bunch of the whiskey-maddened cowboys from rival spreads, punches whirling, glasses smashing, as they snarled and scrimmaged like a pack of vicious dogs.

Anderson grabbed the ringleader by the scruff of his neck, bludgeoning him with the butt of his revolver, and booting him out of the door. 'Go cool off up the road in Rosy Joe's, boys,' he gritted out, handing them their guns. 'You've had your fun. See ya tomorrow night.'

When it had quietened down, Jo remarked, 'You handled that well, Marshal.'

'Yeah, but what worries me is that this is only the start.' He sank the remains of his beer. 'What happens when the other herds arrive? How long does this hullabaloo go on for? When do they start shooting at me?'

'Think of it as money, Marshal.'

'Yeah? Money ain't much good to a man if he's dead.' He jammed on his hat. 'Oh, well, guess I'd better go take a look at the rest of the town. God knows when I get my sleep.'

'Think positive, Marshal,' Jo called. 'You're doing fine.'

If the citizens whined about losing their sleep due to the rowdy cowboys, many of them were coining it in. Abilene was bursting at the seams as professional gamblers, snake-oil salesmen, confidence tricksters, thugs, fakers, bunco steerers and even more girls on the game flocked in on the trains from the East. The Great Western Store was reaping $12,000 a month in sales for Jake Karatovsky, while Tom McKinery employed twenty extra men to replace the drovers' busted boots with fancy high-heeled ones. The first thing the cow-prodders wanted after a summer spent in the saddle was a haircut, shave and hot tub, so there were constant queues outside the barber shop and bath-house. Then they bought some workpants of tough cloth *de Nimes* – or denims – tacked together with rivets, a new shirt and had their pictures taken at a photographer's studio to send home. As more herds arrived, lining up outside town to await their turn to be loaded on to boxcars which went huffing and clanking away along Abilene's main street, bunches of

Texans rode in to enjoy a wild, foot-stomping night of
frontier dancing with the painted cats before return-
ing to their camps. More than a thousand folk
attended the summer race meeting, including five
carriages of so-called soiled doves. They, in their turn,
spent a small fortune on fashion frocks and hats at the
haberdasher's. Meanwhile more settlers were arriving,
ten to fifteen farms a day being sold by the land
agents, and Mayor Hooson lined his pockets with high
profits. Yes, Abilene was one big boom town.

But the farmers were far from happy, especially
those whose land lay in the path of the arriving herds.
Anderson was rudely awakened from sleep one morning by an irate settler and his two brawny sons
hammering on the jailhouse door. Outside on horseback sat the trail boss of the XL Texan spread, a weath-
erbeaten son-of-a-gun in flapping chaps, red
bandanna and beaten-up ten gallon hat.

'His longhorns trampled through our field of corn,'
the farmer cried.

'Yeah.' His son had a shotgun levelled at the trail
boss. 'We've had enough. We want compensation.'

The trail boss tugged at his walrus moustache,
dourly. 'How did I know it was their land? There were
no fences up.'

'You don't need fences in Kansas,' the farmer said.
'State law is you hoe a small trench around what marks
your land. You musta seen it was corn ripe for the
scythe.'

'Yeah, looked mighty appetizing to the cows.' The
trail boss forced a grin. 'You'd better sort this out with

the boss, Mr Herbison. He got here the easy way by steamboat and rail. He's staying at The Cottage.'

'First of all,' Anderson said, 'you can lower that shotgun, son. That's aginst the law. If you refuse it's you I'll be arresting.' He reached in his pocket for his notebook and pencil. 'I want ya names. If this is an official complaint its gotta be done officially.'

He told them to wait in the jailhouse and help themselves to mugs of coffee while he went to locate the rancher. 'We'll get this sorted,' he said. 'No need for gunplay.'

The three-storey Drovers' Cottage was painted bright yellow, with green trim and Venetian blinds. It stood next to the rail depot and had stabling for a hundred horses behind. On its spacious veranda, northern meat-packers and Mid-West feeders made big deals with Texan ranchers, sealing them with handshakes. Anderson stepped inside and peered around its ornate interior. Ladies in long summer dresses and flowered hats were taking morning coffee from silver pots and salvers in the lounge; gentlemen were puffing Havana cigars up at the bar, or clicking balls in the billiards room.

'Is Mr Herbison here?' Anderson asked at the desk.

'He's in a private meeting, sir,' the clerk said. 'He can't be disturbed.'

Anderson tapped at the tin badge on his chest. 'I can disturb who I damn well like.'

A waiter emerged out of a room carrying a tray of brandy glasses. A hubbub of conversation ceased as the marshal pushed in past him. Clarence Hoosen got to his feet. 'You can't come in here, Hank. We're in the middle of important negotations with the railroad boys.'

Anderson was well aware that the Union Central Pacific with its 3000 miles of iron rail had gross revenues the previous year of $17 million and he was dealing with big businessmen. He was unaware that profiteers like the mayor were worried about the new railroad sired by the Atchison, Topeka and – optimistically – Santa Fe company which had a depot at Newton and might well steal the cattle trade. That's what the meeting was about.

'I need to speak to a Mr Herbison,' the marshal said. 'His trail boss is being held in my jail. This is urgent.'

'What's the problem?' A leather Texan in a suit, puffing at a cigar, called out. 'I'm Herbison. Speak up, Marshal.'

Hank outlined the facts. 'The farmer reckons his crop's ruined. He wants a hundred and fifty dollars in compensation.'

'Is that all? Here.' Herbison had just been paid more than $20,000 for his herd. He reached for his wallet, counted out the cash, waved it at Anderson. 'Get him to give you a receipt.'

The rancher then scowled at the others. 'This is one more reason why us drovers might be better advised to sell our herds at Newton or Wichita.'

The problem of farmers having their land trampled was one that would flare up again and again in the summer, a problem that had existed since time began, as Editor Cox put it, since Cain slew Abel, drover versus farmer.

His daughter Jane was very cool and aloof whenever she and Anderson met, which was pretty often as she had to pester the marshal for police news.

One afternoon a prostitute known as Magnificent Mollie, who had been soliciting in the town wearing little else but a long fur coat, which she would flash open to reveal her considerable charms, took it into her head to throw off the fur as it was such a sunny day and strut down the centre of Main Street naked but for black stockings, scarlet garters and her jewellery much to the mirth of idling Texans and cries of horror from starchy, well-covered ladies who were promenading at this busy time of day.

It was Anderson's job to grab hold of the slippery, struggling, giggling girl and drag her away to the hoosegow. 'You'll be up before the beak tomorrow,' he growled, as he locked her in. 'And you'd better keep your damn clothes on.'

Jane seemed to be as shocked as the other church ladies who immediately marched through town behind their discordant brass band singing hymns, demanding that their children be given protection from such sights, and picketing The Longhorn saloon-cum-courtroom with signs saying, 'Thou shalt not sell liquid damnation.'

Magnificent Mollie, other names unknown, was fined five dollars, which Anderson duly entered on his court sheet, along with other drunk and disorderlies he had hauled in.

'Bit of a hoot, ain't she?' he remarked of Mollie as he went through his files for Jane.

'If you find the ruination of a female through drink and prostitution amusing,' she replied tartly, 'that's up to you.'

'You oughta loosen up a bit,' he said. 'Live and let live. When you coming out for a morning gallop with me again?'

'You really think I might *want* to?' she hissed. 'Do you think I like being made a fool of?'

'You still het up about me and Lizzie? We were only having a stroll, that's all.'

'Yes, well I trust you'll enjoy many more strolls with her in the woods.'

'Aw, come on,' he drawled, catching hold of her arm as she gathered up her pencils and notebook and started from the saloon or 'courtroom' door. 'You know it's you I like.'

She spun to face him, her face flushed, her grey eyes flashing. 'Take your hand off me! Do you really think I want to go out with a man who spends most of his time, from what I've heard, in a drinking den and bawdy house of the lowest kind, i.e. Jo's so-called place? In fact, the rumour is you're on that woman's payroll. In other words, Marshal, in my opinion you're nothing but a nasty little pimp and brothel-keeper.'

'Hey!' Anderson had to laugh at her ire. 'You sure got a bee in your bonnet, aincha?' He continued to hold on to her for they were alone and he was half-impelled to drag her into one of the back rooms and have his way with her, or try to, for maybe that was what she wanted. 'OK, I'll tell you the truth,' he said, instead. 'I'm half-owner of that joint. But this is between us. I don't want you printing it in your paper.'

'I thought as much,' she cried, pulling her arm free. 'Don't worry, I won't divulge your dirty secret. Not yet.'

'Chris'sakes, girl, open your eyes. That's what this town's about, making money. And prob'ly, from what I heard today, it ain't gonna be for much longer. So I intend getting a share of the takings while the taking's good. There's nothin' illegal about what goes on at the Devil's Addition. Nothin' you can do about it. So what I do in my spare time after policing this town is my business, as long as it's legal.'

'But why?' She stared at him, blinking back tears. 'I thought you wanted to start a new life, a decent life. Why can't you live on your marshal's salary? Why do you have to sink so low?'

'I'm sorry, Jane. I got different sentiments about this to you. I got what I call my ranch fund. I ain't planning on being a lawman much longer. Soon as I got enough cash put by I'm gonna buy myself a stretch of land. That's the life I want. That's my dream.'

'I see,' she said. 'But, unlike you, I don't believe good can come out of evil.' And she walked out on him.

He stood for a few moments, and shook his head. 'I guess I shoulda grabbed her,' he drawled. 'Respect? Huh! It don't do a man no good.'

*

93

Jo de Merritt was sitting behind her bar the next morning counting the profits as her *filles de joie* sprawled about on horsehair sofas and chairs, combing at their tangled hair, or giving their faces a new coating of flour paste and paint. All *en deshabille*, they had the lassitude of troops after a battle, and Double Barrell Betty was soaking herself in a tub of hot suds on the floor. 'Jeez,' she groaned, 'I musta taken on more'n twenty randy galoots last night. I cain't go on like this, Miss Jo. I'm sore as hell.'

'Put some ointment on it,' the madam muttered, dragging on a cigarette and putting it aside as she continued her count. 'We had a good night, gals. There's gonna be a bonus for y'all.'

'I should damn well think so,' Betty moaned. 'We earned it.'

'Quit whining,' Jo snapped. 'You get to keep your own tips, doncha? Rosy Joe would confiscate 'em all.'

'Talk of the devil!' one of the women exclaimed, for who should come charging through the batwing doors but Rosy himself, a shotgun in his hands.

'I've had enough of this,' he shouted, 'you two-timing whore.' He strode up to de Merritt, his left fist grabbing a handful of her loose and witchlike silver hair, his right sticking the shotgun under her nose. 'Think you can undercut my prices, do you? What's this I hear? Drinks, two fer a quarter? The bitches a dollar a time? What you trying to do? Ruin me?'

'Let me go,' Jo screamed, sticking her nails in his hand, trying to release her hair. It felt like it was being pulled from her head. 'I'll charge what I like.'

'You'll charge what I tell you, you old hag, because from now on I'm taking over this dump. I'm the new owner. See? You got that? You can get out.'

He banged her head on the bar and stepped back, taking a five-dollar bill from his pocket, tossing it under her nose. 'That's what I'm paying. Lock, stock and barrel. The bitches, too. There's a receipt. You sign that, then you can crawl outa here.'

He had been followed into the bar by a young dude, attired in a black velvet shirt, tight black pants and in black, silver-enscrolled boots. His oiled black hair hung down over his forehead and he flicked it aside and gave them all a scoffing grin. 'Howdy, gals,' he crooned, as he stood arms akimbo, fingers touching the twin pearl-handled revolvers, butts forward, hung from the gunbelt around his hips. 'Anybody gonna argue?'

'How about me?' a man's voice drawled from one of the cribs along the wall, and a rifle barrel poked through the drawn curtains.

Joseph Rose spun around towards it. 'What the hell?'

'That's where you'll be headin' pretty soon,' the voice growled, 'if you don't git outa here pronto. And take your dumb sidekick with you.'

Hank Anderson barely remembered falling asleep in the crib. He had hit the whiskey hard, Jane's ultimatum on his mind. He had been woken by the harsh words out in the bar room, and a young trollop called Flash Fanny, half naked beside him, was shaking him by the shoulder.

He parted the curtains of the crib and stepped out, bootless, bare-chested, standing in a faded pair of long drawers. 'You're disturbing my sleep. I don't like that. Makes me feel mean. I don't want to have to take you in again, Joe. This time it won't go so easy. Threatening behaviour, violent assault on a lady. Not nice, Joe.'

'What you doing here?' Rosy Joe had not been expecting this. 'What you taking her side for?'

'Waal, I don't recall you paying me a retainer.' Anderson kept the Creedmore aimed at the big man's chest. The dude was about six feet tall, but slim with it. He had the air of some crazy fast gun, but what the hell. 'I happen to own half-share in this joint and I trust my friend, Miss de Merritt, to run it exactly as she pleases without your say so.'

'You fool, Anderson,' Rosy Joe shouted. 'You think you can take me and Vince here, both? I'm warning you, he's fast.'

'I know one thing, I'll kill you first,' Hank gritted out, 'whatever *he* does.'

'And I'll kill *him*, the handsome li'l sweetheart,' Jo cried, producing a revolver from under the bar, holding it two-handed on the young dude. 'So, I'd advise him to go back to his mammy.'

Rosy Joe stared at them, then jerked his head at Vince to back outside beside him. Joe was ranting and raving obscenities about what he would do to them. 'I'll burn you down,' he roared. 'You can't do this to me.'

'Aw, git lost,' Anderson yelled. 'You don't scare us,

you loudmouth.'

The girls joined in shrieking insults as their madam added, 'Yes, we'll run this place just how we want to. You kill a lawman, Joe, and there'll be no hiding place for you in Kansas.'

'Yes, well, thanks for mentioning that,' Anderson said, after they had gone, helping himself to coffee from the stove. 'Now they'll probably try and back-shoot me in a dark alley.'

He pulled on his pants, boots, his shirt and bandanna, grabbed his hat and growled, 'Guess I'd better git back to work.'

'Aren't you forgetting something, Marshal?' Jo called, dabbing at the bruise on her forehead and waving an envelope. 'Our cut-price offer paid dividends last night.'

'Oh, thanks.' He stuffed the envelope of green-backs into the backpocket of his jeans. 'I'll see ya later.'

At the batwing doors he paused and called out, 'Doncha worry about that drunken loudmouth. It's just a lot of hot air. He won't try anythang.'

He started back for town and glanced warily at Rosy Joe's saloon as he passed. 'At least,' he muttered, 'I hope not. Maybe we shoulda killed both of them when we had the chance. Or tried to.'

NINE

A gang of girls shouted raucously as they spied a small herd of buffalo on the plain. The express train thundered on its way at thirty miles an hour, woodsmoke pouring from its tall stack. 'Go on, mister,' one urged a city dude, who had his rifle raised, taking a pot-shot from the window. 'Git one fer me!'

One of the humpy-backed bison tumbled, setting the others skittering. 'Got him!' the hussy shrieked, hugging the dude and kissing him.

A young boy, Newton Somers, his long, flaxen hair hanging down over his nose, watched wide-eyed. What's the point of that, he wondered. That poor buffalo wouldn't be no good to nobody now. He had heard that the herds had been so decimated there would be few left soon on the southern plains.

But the locomotive's bell was clanging and its whistle blowing as the conductor came along the central aisle. 'Here y'are, sonny. Abilene next stop. Hope you find your kin.'

'I hope so, too, sir,' the boy replied. 'Otherwise, I

don't know what I'll do.'

'Aw, folks won't letcha starve,' the uniformed conductor said, kindly. 'I'd better punch your ticket.'

'I've been wondering,' the boy said. 'Where are all these girls going to?'

'To hell and damnation. And some of 'em ain't much older than you. Good luck, son.'

Newt Somers picked up his small bundle, all he had in the world, apart from a five-dollar note pinned inside the pocket of his church suit. The train was creaking and hissing as it slowed into Abilene and some of the girls were crowding around, preparing to get out to try their luck, as they said. They were squealing farewells to each other. 'Bet I'll make more than you, Lucy,' one of them shouted.

The boy jumped down from the train behind them and watched the gaggle of girls go skipping away through the town. Now he had to try to find his uncle.

Marshal Anderson was sitting in The Longhorn playing a desultory game of poker amid a group of men when the youngster wandered in. 'Hey, kid,' the barkeep shouted. 'You're too young to be in here. Whadda ya want?'

'I want to see Marshal Henry Anderson.'

'Hey, Hank, there's a snotty-nosed brat looking for ya.'

'Come over here, boy,' Anderson called. 'What is it?'

'My mother sent me. Only she's dead now. She said you'd take care of me. You're the only kin I got.'

'*What?*' His mind half-distracted by the cards, Anderson gave the boy a thunderous look. 'What'n hell you talking about? I ain't got no kin.'

'I got a letter,' Newt said, reaching in his pocket. 'I think you're my uncle.'

'Your *what?*' The marshal slapped his cards face down. 'Hang on, boys. I'm out.' He snapped his fingers at Newton. 'Let's take a look at what you got.'

He tore open the envelope the boy offered him and took out a note. In spidery writing were the words: *Hank, for times past take care of Newt for me – Rose.*

For once in his life the marshal looked dumbfounded. 'What's your name, boy?'

'They call me Newt. Newton Somers. Ma wrote that note the day 'fore she died.'

'Rose Somers. What did she die of?'

'The typhoid fever. Grandma's gawn, too.'

'What's this?' Anderson took a news clipping from the envelope.

Under the heading, A HANDSOME PRESENT, it read:

On Monday afternoon Abilene's efficient city marshal, Henry 'Hank' Anderson, was the recipient of a new Winchester rifle of superior workmanship, the barrel octagonal, the stock made of a fine piece of black walnut, and the butt end beautifully engraved and plated with gold. A silver plate inscribed on the stock reads, 'Presented to H. Anderson by his many friends as a reward for services rendered the City of Abilene.' Abilene's mayor, Clarence Hooson, made the presentation and remarked, 'Hank might be a tad quick on the

*trigger but he's tamed this town since I appointed him
to office three months ago. We're all mighty grateful to
him.'*

'Ma cut that out of the *Kansas City Times* a few weeks
ago. She said you were kin of ourn,' the boy put in.
'Does that make sense to you?'

'What's the matter, Hank?' one of the men joshed.
'You look like something nasty's popped outa the
woodwork. Who's the kid? Your past catching up with
you?'

Anderson ignored him. 'How old are you, boy?'

'Ten, sir.'

'Rose Somers?' The marshal appeared lost in
thought. 'So you're her boy? But what you want of me?
I'm a busy man. I ain't got time to bother bringing up
some kid I ain't never met before. Ain't there nobody
else can take you?'

'Ma said you're my only relative.' Newt blinked wide
blue eyes at him. He quickly picked up his bundle and
turned away. 'I don't want to be a burden to you. I can
take care of myself.' At the door he paused and called,
'I'm nearly a man full grown. I'll find myself work
someplace in town.'

Anderson scowled at the men. 'It seems like I got a
nephew.' He got to his feet. 'Newt! Come here, you
idiot. I'm just surprised to see you, thassall. Sit down.
The 'keep'll bring you some grub. I bet you're hungry,
ain't you?'

'It's a long ride from Sedalia, sir, but a lady gave me
some of her lunch.'

'Oh, yeah, in with the ladies, are ya? Don't call me sir. Hank's my handle. Or Anderson. Please yourself. But don't go calling me Uncle, thassall.'

As he drank a glass of beer and watched the boy scoffing his food, he muttered, 'Yeah, I knew Rose ten years ago or so, 'fore I headed West, but I never knew about you. . . .'

'Hiya, Cass,' Anderson called out as he pushed into the jailhouse followed by the boy. 'Everythang quiet?'

'Could say. Found Mad Mick Ryan lying in an alley behind the Bull. He's back there. Certified dead by the coroner. No sign of physical injury. His verdict was alcohol poisoning.'

The town committee had appointed Cassius Clayton deputy marshal a few days before. He was a young, raw-boned, blond fellow, more farmer than gunfighter. A bit wet behind the ears, but he had a wife and family and needed the $50 a month.

'This here's Newt Somers, kin of mine. He's here for a summer holiday – uh – maybe longer. Take a seat over there, Newt.'

Anderson took a look at the corpse. 'Poor ol' Mick. He's well-pickled. Better ask the undertaker to pick him up, Cass, burial at town expense.' He found his log book. 'We have to enter all our deceased in here. See?' He sat down, dipped a pen and started to fill in the appropriate columns. 'Cause of death. What shall we say? "Too much whiskey." Yep, that'll do. Anythang else?'

'I hung around Horse Thieves' Corner, like you

said, checked for the brands and descriptions of missing animals. Found that slate-blue mule stolen from Hagerty's a month ago. The dealer claimed he paid good money for it. I warned him he might well be prosecuted and took it back to the owner – ornery stubborn brute.'

'Who, the mule or Hagerty?'

'Both!' Cass laughed. 'All he said was, "It's taken you long enough to recover".'

'We'll know next time. Let the dealer damn well sell it.' The marshal crossed the mule off the list. 'Now here's one worth going after. A reward of five hundred dollars offered by Captain Nipp for the return of a fine stallion. Must be some horse. You fancy going after him, Cass?'

'But aren't we too busy, Marshal?'

'Aw, I can manage. The captain might have some ideas on who's stolen him. You could take a sniff around the remudas of the Texans. But if there's any threat come and get me. Start tomorrow. Take as long as you like.'

Anderson figured his deputy could do with the reward cash and, to tell the truth, he would be glad to get him out from under his feet. He needed to attend to his own interests down at The Addition. Nor was he so sure that if it came to gunplay the inexperienced farm boy might be more hindrance than help.

'Take the rest of the day off, Cass,' he called. 'Go relax with the wife and kids.'

'Gee, thanks, Hank. I'll be back tonight to give you back-up on the rounds.'

'Nah, have the night off. I can manage. Anyway, I got a new assistant now. Me an' Newt will stick up a few of these town ordinances to let the committee know we're doing our job.'

When his deputy had gone Anderson tidied up his desk and said, 'He's a good man is Cass. A bit too good for this job.'

'What do you mean?' the boy piped up. 'How can you be too good?'

'Well, to do this job you need to know how a bad man thinks. You need to have ridden the other side of the line. Cass told the citizens' committee he can handle a gun. But only years of experience and instinct can tell you when one of these rattlers is likely to strike. Even then, too often you can be caught off guard.'

'Have you ridden the other side of the line?'

Anderson slumped in his swivel chair and lit a cheroot. 'Thangs were hard in the war. Bad done on both sides. It ain't worth dwellin' on. And afterwards? Yeah, I guess I did. But these days I try to ride a straight line. Sorta.' He blew out a smoke ring, watched it waft across the jailhouse. 'It ain't allus easy.'

He studied Newt's innocent, fresh face, met his bright blue eyes. 'You're the spittin' image of your ma. You know that?'

'I got her picture here.' Newt dug in his small bag and brought out a Bible. 'There.'

The studio photograph was stuck inside the front cover. 'Golly gee,' Anderson mused. 'She sure didn't alter much in ten years. Just as purty as she was last time I set eyes on her 'fore the Rebs took me away.' He shook his head, sadly. 'But it seems a long time ago. Tell me, did Rose, your mother, ever git wed?'

'No. But Grandma did, when I was a babe, Ma said. After Granddad got kilt. Grandma needed a man to run the farm. Mr Bass he was called. Ma refused to take his name. She said she would keep her own. We didn't like him. He was a brute, horrible to the horses and animals.'

'Yeah? Rose wouldn't have liked that. She was very sensitive to suffering. Was this fella Bass horrible to you, too?'

'It was the way he bullied Ma, jeered at her ideas, I didn't like. He used to larrup me with his belt if I was slow off the mark or spilt the milk. But I guess I deserved that.'

'Maybe I should go look up this Mr Bass one day . . .'

'Too late now. He died in the epidemic. He was the first to go, close followed by Grandma and Ma. She told me to go 'fore it got me, too.'

Anderson studied the penned inscription under the photograph: *To my beloved son, Newton. If you heed the words of Jesus you will not go far wrong.*

The marshal nodded, silently. 'Rose taught me to read with this Good Book and that book of poems she had. She was a fine girl.'

'That's not what Mr Bass said. He called me names, too, said we were both no good.'

'Sounds to me like this Mr Bass was a dunder-headed fool. You can forget him, Newt.' To divert the boy from such melancholy talk Anderson got up and reached for his new rifle. 'Here's the Winchester they gave me. Nice, ain't it? See the inscription.'

'Wow! Are those bits real gold?'

'Yep. You can hold it. It ain't loaded. The latest model, a 16-shot. To tell the truth I prefer my old Creedmore. All that flashing gold draws attention to a man.'

'It must be worth a fortune.'

'A tidy bit.'

'The committee must think a lot of you, Hank.'

'In my opinion I do believe they were trying to get round me. We had an altercation on account of a little business enterprise I got. I told them where to stick their job. I guess this was their way of wooing me back. To tell the truth I doubt if it cost the mayor and his gang anythang. They'd pay for it outa town taxes. Still, I guess that sounds ungrateful. It's a fine rifle.'

As he watched the boy raise it to his shoulder, Anderson drawled, 'It's a tad heavy for you, but maybe you could use it.'

'I—' Newt laid the rifle aside. 'I ain't allowed. Ma said guns are bad. She said it weren't right to shoot critters just for fun.'

'Your mother had some good feelings, maybe too good. Out here in this wild country there's some critters just have to be shot to protect the community, mainly two-legged ones. Ah, well, if you don't want it I'll stick it back up on its hooks. Looks good, don't it?'

They spent the afternoon tacking up various wordy ordinances aimed at preventing the lighting of bonfires or letting off of squibs – fire among the tinder-dry frame houses was always a threat – or prohibiting 'noisy, riotous, threatening and drunken behaviour', or running horses or wild animals in the town streets or 'lassoing any such animals or persons . . .'

Then there was another law to ban houses of ill fame within the town limits threatening fines of between $10 and $200 for prostitution or 'disorderly, obscene, lewd, profane or indecent conduct'. The girls arrested for such violations generally paid up cheerfully; in fact, so many were fined that summer it paid for the marshal and deputy's salaries.

But the main prohibition was against the firing of guns or carrying of 'deadly weapons, revolvers, muskets, dirks, bowie knives or carbines' with a penalty of ten days in jail and a fine for those who flouted the rule. Just how the town marshal was meant to arrest them was not stated.

Anderson was up a ladder nailing a large sign to a telegraph pole stating ALL GUNS TO BE HANDED IN when a gang of newly arrived Texans came cantering by, whooping and shouting, brandishing their revolvers and riddling the sign with holes, making the lawman leap from the ladder for safety.

Newt tried to hang on to the ladder but it toppled over as the Texans rode by laughing. 'You OK, Mr Anderson?' he asked.

'Yeah.' Anderson recovered his hat and watched the horsemen dismount outside The Bull. 'We got plenty of laws in this town, but there ain't a lot of order.'

The scruffy gang of cowhands were grinning at him,

mockingly. 'Stay here, boy,' Anderson muttered, and loosened his own Remington as he strode across.

'Hold it right there,' he called. 'I oughta toss the whole gang of you in the calaboose. But I'm just gonna warn you. Hand in all your guns to my office, or the main stores, or at the saloon doors. You can collect 'em when you leave town.'

'Who's gonna make us?' one of the gang jeered.

'C'mon, boys.' A taller Texan they called Slim intervened. 'Don't give the marshal no hassle. He's only doing his job. Hand your gunbelts in at the door. Or we won't be served no whiskey.'

The thirsty cowboys clattered, spurs jingling, into the bar, but one of them, a rough-looking young *hombre*, Joel by name, leered at Anderson. 'Who the hell makes these laws?'

'If you could read you'd see they're signed "By order of the mayor".'

'That so. And just who is the mayor?'

It so happened that the chubby Clarence Hooson had come out of his bank to sun himself on the sidewalk, beaming unctuously at passers-by as he rubbed his chubby hands.

'Well, as a matter of fact, that's him over there.'

'That so?' Joel leapt on his pinto, hurtled across the wide, dusty street, twirling his lariat and neatly lassoed the mayor. He jerked the rope tight around his shoulders and set off down towards The Addition. At fast speed he dragged the mayor bumping and struggling on his backside, much to onlookers' merriment and catcalls, and dumped him at the edge of town.

Anderson watched the cowboy charge back and jump to the ground, a defiant grin on his face. 'Very funny,' the marshal drawled. 'You better get lost in the crowd inside 'fore I'm ordered to toss you in the hoosegow.'

Newt, like all the others, found the incident hilarious, cheering when the mayor strutted back, his suit torn and stained with dust and dung. 'Have you arrested him?' Hooson spluttered.

'Nope. He got away. I'll go inside see if I can find out who he was. You better git back in your bank, Mr Mayor, 'fore you come to any more harm.'

'This is outrageous,' the mayor cried, but hurried back across the street to safety.

Anderson pushed into The Bull. It was a rough dive that sold just cheap whiskey and Kansan steam beer. He took a stance at one end of the bar.

'I'm glad to see that y'all seem to have surrendered your guns,' he said to the lanky Slim, who greeted him. 'I'm gonna turn a blind eye to your pal Joel's prank, but any more trouble 'n' I'll be forced to take action.'

'Aw, us Texans ain't as bad as we're painted. You got no need to worry about us, Marshal.' Slim was a typical Westerner, a big bandanna hung around his throat. 'We like to get up a li'l racket now and agin, but it's all in fun.'

'Yep, well, you can tell your pal the only reason he ain't behind bars is 'cause I've done enough paperwork for today.'

'Don't blame you, Marshal,' Slim replied, offering

Anderson a whiskey. 'Like the great General Forrest said, most of us would sooner pick up a snake than a pen.'

Anderson smiled, grimly, for the Texan was obviously testing his loyalties. He raised the whiskey. 'I'll drink to that. A good man. He oughta have been president of the Confederacy, not that tinhorn lawyer, Davis'

Newt was waiting for him outside. It was getting late. 'You'll have to bed down in the jailhouse tonight. But don't you go near any of the prisoners, boy, while I'm away, however they try to cajole you. They'll try to git you to give 'em the keys.'

He had a couple of horse-thieves awaiting trial, and a drunk sleeping it off. He fed and watered them and found the boy a cot and blankets. 'You just read your Good Book and don't unlock to nobody 'til I get back,' he instructed, buckling on his gunbelt and reaching for a spare box of .44s, loading his Remington revolver and checking its action. 'I gotta go out. I should be back sometime after midnight.'

'Can't I come with you?'

'Nope. The saloons this time of night ain't suitable sights for a boy.' He almost added that they could be dangerous. And, as he looked at Newt, he realized that for the first time in his life there was someone he was responsible for. He met the boy's trusting eyes and ruffled his hair. 'Take it easy, kid.'

TEN

Beware, sinners, the placard held by the old man warned, *your time is nigh.*

'Yeah, thanks for reminding me,' Anderson drawled, as he stepped by the crazy Bible thumper who took his stand on the corner of Texas Street most nights.

It was Saturday night and the joints were jumping, music and laughter bursting from the doors of the saloons and beer parlours. He had checked them all by eleven o'clock, just stepping inside to watch goings-on for a while. He had even shown his face in The Drover's Cottage and chatted to the legendary Joe McCoy. 'You're doing a good job, Marshal,' he said. 'Don't let us down.'

Just what did he mean by that? Hank wondered, as he swung on his way, looking in at The Alamo, then on to Hyram Hunnisegger's billiards parlour, Had the promoter heard about his connections with the sleazier side of life?

'Hell,' he muttered, 'McCoy's made his millions.

111

Why shouldn't I have a slice?'

But for some reason he felt uneasy this night as he headed downhill towards The Devil's Addition. He glanced up warily at the false fronts silhouetted against a clear summer sky. He wouldn't put it past Rosy Joe to have a sniper lurk up on one and take a bead on him one of these nights. So far Joe Rose had suffered the indignity of Anderson's support for a rival only fifty yards away, but every time the marshal spotted him he could tell the saloon-keeper was seething with supressed fury. One of these days Rosy Joe's anger might well explode.

Anderson tensed to see Vince, the dude in black, standing on the porch outside Joe's bawdy house as he walked by.

'Waal, look who's here,' the gunslinger sang out to a couple of pals beside him. 'Our fine upstanding law officer.'

'Maybe he won't be so upstanding for much longer,' one of his cronies jeered. 'Know what I mean?'

Anderson turned to take a stand in front of them, his hand hovering over his holstered Remington. 'You boys want somethang with me? If so, spit it out.'

'No, not yet, we don't.' Vince tossed his hair from his eyes with a toothy grin. 'We're biding our time.'

Anderson shrugged and walked on past the two rows of huts, or cribs, where a flock of freelance arrivals had settled in and were doing good business.

'Live and let live,' the marshal muttered, ' 'cause there sure ain't no shortage of punters this time of the year.'

'That young Vince has got more airs than a spotted stud horse in a county fair ring,' Miss Jo complained when he stepped into the former First or Last Chance. 'He was in here earlier strutting his stuff, making threats.'

'Yeah, like what?'

'He just said that Rosy Joe ain't one to forget. But it was the way he said it, spinning them twin pearl handles of his, showing us just how fast he can draw.'

'I'm ready for him.' The place was packed, hot, and smelling of alcohol, tobacco fumes, nauseous whale oil lamps, and human sweat, male and female. He was mildly surprised to see the Texans from that afternoon's shindig. The lasso-spinner, Joel, was hopping about midfloor with Double-Barrel Betty in his arms. The lanky Slim was leaned back against the bar and winked at him.

'Your pal's still full of high spirits.'

'Aw, he's OK. Just enjoying the party.'

The marshal went behind the bar. 'How's it going?' His partner had bought a bulldog, maybe to be one-up on Big Kate and it growled, malevolently. 'Not too bad, but not so good, either. Your share's two hundred dollars this week.' Jo de Merritt slid an envelope along to him. 'It ain't as much as I promised you, I know, but we've got a lot of competition and overheads.'

'Like what?'

'Here, see for yourself. 'The silver-haired madame opened a leather-bound accounts book. 'It's all there in black and white. The gals' share, payments for beer and whiskey deliveries, replacement crockery that gets smashed. The boys in the band don't play for free. I ain't holding out on you, Hank.'

He checked the figures. 'I didn't say you were. Who's complaining?'

'Good.' Jo snapped the book shut. 'So relax. You know, you and me could make a great team if we got hitched.'

Anderson grinned with surprise. 'You proposin' to me, Jo? Ain't you a bit long in the tooth for that?'

'What's a few sags and wrinkles, Marshal? You might find out I can be pretty slick between the sheets. You might be pleasantly surprised. A woman my age is in her prime.'

'I'll bear it in mind.' Anderson went back into the main body of the saloon and stood at the bar, drinking a beer and chatting to the Texan, Slim. Suddenly he noticed three men at a table on the far side of the hall. One of them wore a brown frock coat trimmed with velvet and the marshal had a feeling he hadn't deposited his ironwear at the door. There was something familiar about him, his long-nosed, clean shaven face beneath his wide-brimmed hat. He was no Texan, that was for sure. His eyes glimmered like some weasel on the prowl, and he stared intently at the lawman.

'I've seen him before.'

'Henry Anderson,' the man shouted in a stentorian tone, making the dancers grind to a halt. 'I've been looking for you a long time.'

Suddenly he remembered and it was as if a coldness shivered through him. The man behind the Gatling gun. The man with his finger on the trigger, a manic

114

look in his eyes as he started to mow down the surrendering Rebs. Abel McKenzie!

His two companions were attired like him, one heavily bearded, the other with a prickly pencil moustache, both smartly suited with frock coats, which covered the tell-tale bulges of concealed weapons. And both were reaching to bring them out. 'You're one of Quantrill's murdering bastards,' McKenzie screamed. 'Die!'

Anderson knew in a flash that he hadn't a hope in hell of beating all three, but he drew his Remington almost simultaneously as McKenzie produced his Colt revolver. Both guns crashed out.

Double-Barrel Betty screamed as Joel toppled her to the floor, brought a knife from out of his boot, and hurled it at the bearded one. The steel penetrated deep in the man's belly, made him misjudge his shot, and the bullet slammed into Betty, instead. She screamed some more.

In the few seconds that McKenzie had taken to shout out his words, Jo de Merritt had brought her revolver out from under the bar, fumbling to cock it. Slim snatched it from her, raised it with experienced hands, aimed double-handed, and his slug sent Prickly Moustache somersaulting backwards out of his chair.

Their help gave Anderson the chance to thumb his revolver's hammer a second time and his lead smashed into The Beard's face, disintegrating it in a mess of blood and bone.

As the acrid gunsmoke drifted away in the ill-lit

room, Anderson saw Abel McKenzie was still sitting in his chair, his maniacal eyes glinting as he stared at him. Then blood spilled from his mouth and his revolver dropped from his lifeless fingers as he slumped back.

'Whee-yo!' the Texan, Slim, whooped. 'That was a close run thang.' He strode across and put another slug in McKenzie's head. 'Just making sure, folks. Never can be sure these cowardly Yankees ain't playin' possum.'

It was not until Anderson saw his blood leaking on to the bar that he knew he had been hit. He had backed up against it and, turning, was surprised to see the bright red drops. 'Where's that come from?'

'What's the matter, Marshal?' Slim smiled, grimly, as he returned. 'We gotta do all your work?'

'Thanks,' Anderson whispered. 'I guess I owe you.'

'You don't owe us nuthin'. I rode with the Texas Brigade. Seems like we were both on the same side.'

'Ar, my God!' Joel was kneeling over Double-Barrel Betty. 'She's day-ed!'

There was a hubbub of commotion as the hurdy gurdy girls and Texans craned to stare at the dead Betty and the bloodily slain men.

'You OK, Marshal?' Miss Jo asked. 'You been hit?'

'That damn McKenzie got me. I'll be all right.'

'Strikes me them three coyotes were men of the feud,' Slim said. 'Their kin may well come looking for you. If you was with Quantrill you've sure chose a funny place to live. War's been over six years, but round these parts feelin's still run high. If it were me

116

I'd be thinkin' of moving on.'

'Yeah.' Anderson gritted his teeth as Jo dosed his wound with whiskey. 'But I've got kin now, too.'

CARNIVAL OF BLOOD! *The Clarion*'s banner headline trumpeted.

In the early hours of Sunday, the Devil's favourite day to operate, the demons of discord were let loose. Riot, blood and murder were rampant in Abilene, leaving three men and one woman dead.

Many blame the Texan men for all the trouble in our town, but the wholesale butchery on Sunday morning was brought about by three Kansans, yet to be identified. When all three drew concealed revolvers and attacked Marshal Hank Anderson without warning, two Texans came to his aid and helped the marshal return fire.

What was the result? Three Kansan horse dealers blasted into eternity and, as always, in gun battles of this kind, one onlooker, Betty Morris, left dying in her own blood. One can hardly call her innocent as she was an inmate of Jo de Merritt's bawdy house where the shootings took place. The dead prostitute was better known by her trade name, Double-Barrel Betty, for what reason only those of vile and sordid mind can imagine.

Marshal Anderson, firing from a sideways stance, received a bullet wound to his back, the lead penetrating the flesh and grazing his right shoulder blade. Luck was on his side, but it is becoming increasingly clear that like his Texan friends, Anderson has the killer instinct, much like his predecessor, Wild Bill.

Why, people are asking, did these three Kansan men come looking for our marshal? It is rumoured that they were former Red Legs, who in the recent conflict protected state borders from the murderous Quantrill Raiders. It is well known that Anderson hails from Missouri. Could it be that he harbours some dark secret that invited a grudge attack?

One thing is clear: Abilene welcomes all honest folk to our fine town. But those desirous of an early death, or merely wishing to be gulled and robbed, should visit the Devil's Addition.

'Strong stuff,' the marshal drawled, as he read the report at the bar of The Longhorn. 'Old Aaron Cox is putting the hounds on my scent.'

'Why?' The barkeep Jim looked uneasy as he refreshed his coffee cup. 'Is it true what they're saying, that you rode with Quantrill.'

'What if I did?' Anderson growled. 'Those Red Leg scum shot Jesse James when he rode in with us boys under a white flag to surrender. Luckily for him and me we got away. The others weren't so lucky. They were mown down by a concealed machine-gun. The war's over. Ain't it time to call it quits?'

'Some will never forget nor forgive,' Jim said, 'what Quantrill and his men did.'

'That's pretty clear. Maybe I was a fool to think they would,' Anderson said. 'But I ain't running. Not just yet.'

He winced at the wound that had creased his back.

Doc Rosen had bandaged him up, but it felt like it had opened again, that blood was sticking to his shirt. 'Hot damn,' he growled. 'I ain't leaving 'til I got a good grubstake outa this unholy town.'

'Hello!' Jane smiled with surprise when she called into the jailhouse the morning after the killings and saw the blond-haired boy sitting in the marshal's swivel chair. 'What are you doing here?'

'Anderson's over at The Longhorn having his pick-me-up,' Newt replied. 'I'm looking after things here. I got strict instructions not to go near any of them varmints in the cells, so if you want to visit them you'll have to wait, ma'am.'

'I'm unmarried so it's miss.' Jane's smile widened at the pipsqueak's air of authority. 'Anderson? Is that what you call him. Who are you? His new deputy?'

'You could say.' The boy grinned, disarmingly. 'He told me to call him that 'cause he don't like the name Hank. Says it's too familiar. I'm his kin. I arrived on the train yesterday.'

'His kin?' Jane studied Newt, quizzically. 'Do you realize your friend Anderson might well have been killed last night? What would you have done then?'

'I don't know, miss. But he wasn't, was he? It was them three badmen who got killed.'

'How about his wound?'

'Aw, he says that's nuthin'. Just a crease.'

'Call me Jane.' The reporter elicited more information from the boy. A lot more. 'So, that's how it is,' she murmured. 'Well, I think it's high time he found you a proper place to live and enrolled you in school.'

'No.' The boy made a grimace of distaste. 'He wouldn't want to do that. Anderson's gonna buy me a pony and teach me to shoot. I'm gonna be a marshal just like him.'

ELEVEN

'A gun ain't a toy,' Anderson growled. 'You gotta treat it with respect at all times. You allus remember that, Newt.'

They were down by the riverside a few days later. The boy was giggling with joy as he managed to hold the new Winchester hard into his shoulder and his fifth shot smashed a bottle on a boulder to smithereens.

'This ain't a game,' Anderson warned, as he gave the ten-year-old his first lesson in shooting. 'This is deadly serious.'

He had bought the boy a ten-dollar cow pony because he figured it was time he learned to ride and togged him out in a pair of denim jeans and shirt, a bandanna and wide-brimmed hat to shield his eyes from the fierce sun. The pinto pony had a smoky eye but was a sturdy mount and was grazing now loose-hitched alongside the grey mare. 'He don't seem to be gun-shy which is a good thing. The mare will settle him.'

121

'Yeah,' the boy cried. 'They seem to be the best of pals. Whoo, this is heavy! Can I put it down now?'

'You gotta get used to holding it. It will strengthen your wrists.' Anderson perched a bottle on a rock a bit further away. 'See if you can hit that. You only got a coupla slugs left. Then I'll show you how to reload.'

The sound of gunfire brought Jane Cox galloping towards them on her chestnut. 'What on earth is going on?' she cried. 'Are you teaching this innocent to be a killer like you?'

'I'm teaching him to defend himself,' the marshal said. 'That's all the schooling he needs in these parts.'

'You made me *miss*,' the boy put in. 'But I got one bottle just now, Jane. Anderson's given me his rifle. Ain't it a beauty?'

In her purple hat and riding habit, Jane sat her chestnut and frowned at the gold-trimmed Winchester. 'It's a man's rifle, not a boy's.'

'Who asked you here, anyhow?' Anderson was not best pleased with the Coxs due to the headlines that had blared from their rag the previous day: ABILENE'S MARSHAL RODE WITH QUANTRILL RAIDERS! and the sub-head, *After war with notorious Wilcox gang in New Mexico.*

Yeah, the shit had sure hit the fan. Anderson had been beseiged in his jailhouse by a mob wanting to know if it were true. 'Sure it's true,' he told them, shrugging them off as he pushed through them. 'But I'm staying in office until I'm voted out. So you better get off the streets, or I might be forced to arrest one or two of you.'

'I was told I might find you out here,' Jane said,

stepping down without invitation.

'You wanna make sure I ain't been lynched?'

'That was not the intention of that article. We were simply telling the truth. I'm here because I want you to give us your side of the story. A full interview.'

So it'll put up your sales.'

'Come on, Marshal, don't be bitter,' she coaxed. 'Wouldn't it be best to clear the air, make a clean breast of things?'

'What's the point in that? A man cain't alter what's been done. If I tell you what I did it ain't gonna bring back them people in Lawrence that I killed. I didn't want no part of that massacre. It sickened me, but I was forced to take part,' Anderson muttered, staring at the river's whorls, as if deep in thought. 'No, that ain't true, I wasn't forced. I took part willingly. But I didn't kill no wimmin or kids.'

Jane spoke more gently to him. 'As I understand it you weren't much more than a kid yourself when they shot your stepfather and press-ganged you into their ranks?'

'I was old enough to know right from wrong. I believed it was my duty to fight for the South. I ain't the only one.'

'How about in New Mexico?'

'I fell in with a bad bunch. When Wilcox got gunned down the governor gave us a free pardon. I ain't on the run or nuthin'. So, what else you want to know!'

Jane sat down on a boulder and pulled out her notebook and pencil. 'I just want people to hear it in your own words, that's all.'

'My side of the story, huh? OK, I'll fill in a few details you got wrong. But this ain't gonna be no sob story. I don't give a cuss what folks think.'

Jane listened to his words, jotting down notes, and finally remarked, 'What I don't understand is why you came back to Kansas at all. Lawrence is only two stops away along the line.'

'Maybe I wanted to face buzzards like McKenzie. Maybe I wanted to have it out.' Anderson grinned at her. 'They say confessin' is good for the soul. Funny, I do feel a lot lighter fer gittin' all that off my chest.' He strolled over to his mare. 'You comin' for a ride with us?'

'Hank,' she called, when she was mounted, 'why don't you drive me to church tomorrow and face the whole town?'

'No, thanks. I don't believe in all that garbage. If God did make man in his own image he sure did make one hell of a mess of thangs. . . . Come on, Newt. Show me what pace that pony's got.'

He's a strange man, Jane thought, as she chased away after them along the river-bank.

When the profile appeared in *The Clarion,* folks, even the town committee, seemed to agree that the marshal should stay in his job. It was a hectic time of year so who else could they get? And he had done his duty well so far.

As Aaron Cox proclaimed: *The glory of Kansas is that all men are welcomed to this thriving new state no matter what their past. If they are brave, hard-working and honest they will be counted one of us.*

So Anderson continued with his mundane tasks, like the arrest of two tricksters who had convinced a gullible farmer that gold-painted lead pieces were twenty-dollar eagles. When they couldn't pay the fine they were put in leg irons clearing rubbish from the streets at two dollars a day until it was paid.

One evening he saw the flashy gun-toter, Vince, come charging through the crowded main street on an even flashier black stallion. He heard a girl's shrill scream and caught a glimpse of Lizzie hanging on behind, her arms clutched around Vince's waist. The rider swerved around a wagon, ploughed through a gang of children and dogs in a cloud of dust, and disappeared around the corner of the houses. Anderson leaped on his mare and set off in pursuit.

The mare's hoofs thudded rythmically on the hard prairie as the marshal gradually caught up. When Vince glanced back and saw him coming he pulled one of his pearl-handled Smith & Wesson's and fired wildly into the air, making the girl scream some more.

'What's the matter, Marshal?' Vince grinned, as he turned the stallion to face him. 'You got a message for us?'

'I sure have.' Vince still had his revolver in his hand, but not pointed his way. So Anderson took out his notebook and licked his pencil stub. 'Just gimme your full name. You'll be up before the court charged with fast riding. You damn fool, you coulda killed one of those kids back there.'

'Sure, but I didn't, did I? My handle's Vincent Santa Cruz.'

'You sure don't look very saintly to me.'

'You know *my* name, Marshal, don't you?' Lizzie's hat had fallen to hang on her back and her blonde hair was blowing across her face in the wind. She hung on to Vince and smiled, enticingly. 'You ain't gonna tell my pa, are you?'

'Maybe he oughta know you're gettin' into bad company. This guy ain't no good for you, Lizzie. He's trouble.'

'What's really buggin' you, Marshal?' Vince gave his mocking grin. 'Maybe you're jealous Lizzie's being given a ride by somebody more her own age.'

'Yes,' Lizzie simpered. 'Why should that worry a wonderful Quantrill Raider?'

'I didn't know those scum,' Vince drawled, '*worried* about anybody.'

'Put that gun away.' Anderson circled the black stallion. 'I'm taking you in on suspicion this hoss is stolen.'

'You're a laugh a minute, Marshal.' Vince spun the revolver with fancy speed and returned it to his left-hand holster. He obviously favoured the cross-hand draw. 'You cain't prove a damn thing.'

Vince was right. The brand on the stallion didn't tally with that of Captain Nipp's missing one, and it didn't appear to have been tampered with. So he got off with a fine of five dollars for fast riding.

An uneasy truce reigned between Rosy Nose Joe

and Anderson whenever he visited the Devil's Addition. Neither establishment was taking the proceeds it had expected to, but Jo de Merritt continued to provide the marshal with a tidy sum in an envelope each week.

One night he took out a ten-dollar bill and offered it to Cass, who was accompanying him on his rounds.

'What's that for?' the deputy asked.

Anderson shrugged. 'I got an interest in this joint. It pays well.'

'No.' Cass pushed his arm away. 'I don't take bribes.'

'It ain't a bribe: it's *my* money. Only I got plenty and you ain't, so here. Treat the wife.'

'No.' Cass shook his head stubbornly. 'I don't want it, Marshal. I ain't treading that path.'

Anderson shrugged again and returned the bill to his envelope. 'All the more for my fund.'

'What fund?'

'I ain't gonna be a lawman much longer, Cass. I don't like this job. I'm thinkin' of headin' for California, buy me some land, run a few cows.'

'We better go take a look in The Bull, Hank. Do they pay you in there, as well'

'You got me all wrong, Cass. But I tell you what, why don't you and the missus join me for dinner in The Alamo one night? It'd be on the house.'

They never did keep that date but Anderson sometimes took Newt out for a meal with the Claytons at their rundown smallholding. Cassius obviously idolized his wholesome young wife and their two children. 'I envy them their happiness,' he said one night, as they rode back to the jailhouse.

Newt pricked up his ears. 'You could be happy, too. Why don't you marry Jane?'

Anderson laughed. 'Because she ain't asked me!'

Between them the two lawmen managed to keep Abilene marginally law-abiding as the rambunctious cattle town went about its business. But in mid-August when Anderson took a look in the Drovers' Cottage he found the bar being dismantled, the bottles crated up, the dining-room closed.

'I'm taking the whole place down and moving to Newton,' Joe McCoy explained. 'You may think this town's bursting at the seams, but we ain't had the business we've had in previous summers.'

He waved a cigar over at the stockyards by the rail depot, where cattle were bellowing plaintively. 'We may look busy but the ranchers are favouring Newton and Wichita now. It's ironic to think I built this city outa nuthin', I invented the cattle business as it is today, but now I got to follow the herds. Still, I can assure you, Marshal, even in Newton the Drovers' Cottage will still be the real McCoy. I ain't one to miss out.'

They say Abilene is quietening down, Aaron Cox remarked in his column, aiming at a bit of sardonic humour. *To be sure it is fast relapsing into morality. There are only ten saloons, thirty gamblers, eighty cowboys and sixty prostitutes in the entire town. Some might say we are going to the Devil, but most God-fearing citizens will be glad to hear*

*that our two law-enforcers are fast getting rid of that element
that has proved a curse to our prosperity. Let those who dare,
go to bloody Newton as it is fast becoming known – nine men
were killed or wounded in a saloon fracas there only last week
– Abilene will always be the cowboy capital of the USA!*

How wrong could he be? Soon, cattle arriving had
dwindled to a trickle, and the wide, dusty street had
almost the look of a ghost town compared to what had
been. The painted courtesans, gamblers and conmen
had gone, too, either to Newton or Wichita, or back
on the railroad to work the Mississippi riverboats
down to New Orleans. The majority of the beer
parlours, cribs and saloons were shuttered-up. Knots
of hard-up cowboys hung about on the sidewalks, or
found jobs painting houses, but most had drifted back
to Texas.

A million cattle had been herded through Abilene
since its inception but from now on, although Aaron
Cox did not yet know it, the main loading points
would be – for a violent year or two – Newton, Wichita
or Caldwell, until, as the iron rails pushed further
West, Dodge City would blaze a mean reputation of its
own.

Now, on an early September day Abilene seemed
uncannily quiet. But not for long. . . .

TWELVE

Rosy Joe, his Lincoln hat perched jauntily, sat in a rocker on the stoop of his bawdy house and watched Anderson and Cass Clayton ride past and out of town. His information was that they were going south for a few days to search for Captain Nipp's missing stallion.

'Right.' He nodded at the two hard men in range clothes, toting iron, who lounged on upturned barrels beside him. 'We'll give 'em time to git well away then we'll hit.'

'You sure about this?' Ben Watson had been a ne'er-do-well villain for most of his adult years. His surly features rarely expressed anything but bad temper. 'We don't wanna be doing this fer peanuts.'

' 'Course I'm sure,' Big Joe growled. 'There's twenty thousand in that vault just beggin' to be shared 'tween the four of us.'

John Wesley, optimistically named after the preacher, was a younger man whose sharp, pallid face split readily into a leering grin, but it was a smile that often inspired fear. He idly held the gutta-percha grip of a Peacemaker six-gun with a four-and-three-quarter-inch barrel. 'Five thou' each.' He gave a whistle of awe. 'That don't sound bad.'

He raised the single action and, squinting through one eye, aligned the knifeblade front sight with the rear's v-channel, and took a pot at a stray dog poking into some rubbish. The cur leapt for cover, howling its fear, and Wesley cackled with laughter. 'Missed!'

As the explosion echoed away Rosy Joe thundered, 'You damn fool. You wanna bring the marshal back here?'

'So? I ain't sceered of him if you is, Joe.' Wesley let the revolver hang between his fingers. 'What we waitin' fer? Let's go.'

'Shut up!' Joe roared. 'Just watch what you're doing. I told ya, I don't want no killing on this job. We just walk in and when Hooson sees us he'll be so scared he'll shit his pants. We just scoop what's there and git out fast. OK?'

'Sure,' Ben Watson nodded. 'How could Wes hit a barn door with that li'l barrel? He ain't gonna kill nobody.'

'The reason I got four inches is so I can stuff this gun in my coat pocket,' John Wesley explained, 'so nobody knows I'm toting iron.'

'Pah!' Watson spat out a gob of chewed baccy. 'Four inches is prob'ly more'n that other li'l thang you got hanging 'tween your legs. Man needs a good nine inches like mine.'

Rosy Joe had paid off his *houris*, finished off most of his beer and whiskey, and locked up the joint in case he didn't come back. He scratched at his purple-veined, bulbous nose and said, 'Come on, let's make our move.'

Fifteen minutes later they rode slowly into the quiet town and, as arranged, found Vince Santa Cruz leaning against the clapboard wall of a store adjacent to Abilene City Bank, his arm around Lizzie Upstone.

'What the hell you doing?' Rosy Joe gasped. 'What you got her along for?'

Vince ceased his canoodling, detached his shoulder blades from the wall and stepped close. 'She's coming with us. We're runnin' away to git wed.'

'You crazy?' Ben Watson glowered at the black-clad youth, then pulled his bandanna up over his face. 'Come on,' he growled, climbing from his horse. 'What we waiting for?'

Rosy Joe looked around. At this midday hour most folks had gone off to eat or take a break and the bank appeared to be devoid of customers. 'Good,' he said, stepping down, gripping his shotgun. 'Let me in the back.' He removed his top hat and stuffed it in one of his saddle-bags, and hurried round to the rear door by the coal shed. In the shadow of the bank he donned a black cash-bag mask with slits for the eyes and mouth, and waited.

Vince took Lizzie's arm and pushed her before him into the bank. 'Wait over there, honey,' he said in a pleasant tone. 'I'm just gonna draw out some cash.'

Clarence Hooson looked up from his ledger with a smarmy smile on his face as he peered through his grille at the new customer. 'Yes, can I help you, sir?'

'You sure can.' Vince scorned to wear a mask and grinned amiably at the banker. 'Just hand over the keys to the vault and don't try nuthin'. OK?'

Hooson's face froze as he gazed behind Vince and saw the two other men, only their eyes revealed beneath the brims of their Stetsons and their bandannas drawn up above their nostrils. He glanced at the frightened girl in her pink polkadot dress and straw bonnet, and checked the deathly holes of the two men's revolvers aimed at him.

Vince had his hands free, his black hair hanging over his brow, just smiling expectantly at the banker. Maybe Hooson couldn't bear to part with all of his cash, but he opened a drawer and came out with a snub-nosed Colt Storekeeper, fumbling to hold it with his sweating, pudgy palms, to thumb the hammer, aiming it at Vince.

Quick as a flash Santa Cruz snatched his left pearl-handled Smith & Wesson from its greased holster with his right hand, fired with the ease of the experienced gunslinger and, as the shot crashed out, before Hooson could squeeze the trigger of his Storekeeper, a .44 slug hit him in the chest like a red-hot rod of iron.

The banker staggered back, blood flowering upon his starched shirt, staring at them aghast, then desperately tried to reach the time switch to lock the vault for eight hours solid. But his fingers clawed in vain as a second shot rang out and lead severed his spine.

Vince stood there, still grinning, a gun now in each fist, both barrels smoking. As he did so the bank teller,

Horace Geppert, stepped out from a back room, his hands in the air. Ben Watson immediately fired his nine-inch barrel Frontier and the bullet hit Geppert between the eyes, demolishing his brain.

Rosy Joe was hammering on the back door. 'Go let him in,' Watson muttered through his neckerchief.

'What you doing,' the masked Joe howled, surveying the two dead bodies on the floor. 'I told you to wait for me. I told you *no killin'.*'

'The fat fool drew on me,' Vince snapped, going to calm Lizzie who looked like she was about to have a screaming fit.

'Where are his keys?' Joe shouted from out of his muffling cash-sack.

Wesley had vaulted the counter and was rummaging through drawers, stuffing spare silver and notes into his pockets as he did so. 'Here!' he said, and jumped over Hooson's prone, bleeding body to open the vault. 'Wow! Jest look at this. Aladdin's cave. Boys, we're rich.'

'Keep us covered, Vince.'

Lizzie was trembling all over. 'What are you doing, Vince?'

'I told ya.' He stuffed away his left-hand gun and gripped her arm so she couldn't run. 'Gettin' some cash. We'll need it for our honeymoon, gal.'

The other three robbers were frantically stuffing wads of greenbacks into the flour sacks they had brought, clearing the shelves of the vault. 'It's more'n a man ever dreamed of,' John Wesley yelled.

'Right, let's go,' Joe ordered, and led the way

outside, two sacks tied at the necks stuffed with loot in one fist, which he slung over the neck of his bronco.

'They're robbing the bank!' a voice boomed, and Rosy Joe turned to see the Revd. Copsey stomping along the sidewalk towards them. His black beard waggled furiously. 'Stop, you villains!'

'Go to hell.' Rosy Joe, past caring now, swung the twelve gauge on the preacherman and blasted out two barrels of shot. 'Go dance with the Devil. See what you been missing!'

Vince was forcing Lizzie to climb on a spare mustang he had brought along. He grabbed its leading rein, pointed a gun at the girl, and shouted at men who had come from shop doorways. 'You fire on us and she's dead.' He grinned mockingly and cantered away, dragging Lizzie alongside him and, as the three other bank-robbers hurtled past on their horses, Vince wildly fired off his remaining bullets at anybody unwise enough to try to stop them. He put spurs to his black stallion, chasing after Joe and his pals.

Terrified, Lizzie hung on to her saddlehorn, trying to stay upright, and glimpsed her father outside his shop, staring with horror as his daughter on her mustang galloped past him.

'Help!' she cried faintly.

About high noon the marshal's grey had cast a shoe and he had turned back for fear she might go lame. A couple of miles from Abilene they heard gunshots barreling towards them across the prairie. 'What's that?' Cass asked, as they spurred their mounts back to town.

Men were buzzing about on horseback trying to organize a posse as they reached the bank. Anderson took one look at the bodies and asked, 'Who was it? Which way did they go?'

'They were wearing masks,' Fin Warren, a cowboy from a small ranch outside town, called. 'But it looked to me like Rosy Joe and his boys.'

Anderson saw Newt among the rubberneckers. 'Go get me the spare mustang from out the stable.'

'Can I come?' the boy asked.

'No, you cain't. Stay here. Take care of the mare.' The marshal raised his hands to quieten the angry crowd. 'We're going after 'em. Any man willin' to join the hunt is welcome, but I'm warnin' you it could be a long chase. Dangerous, too. These boys burn powder without no preliminary talk.'

There was little hesitation. A body of twenty townsmen were quickly mounted and charged out of town hell for leather. It looked like the robbers were heading along the river for Big Bend. But there was little sign of their trail and the posse settled into a steady lope for the rest of the day, gleaning information from the few and far between settlements and travellers they passed.

They had ridden for forty miles when the glowing red ball of sun sank behind the western horizon and darkness fell. Some of the townsmen, shopkeepers unused to hard riding, were about done in and Anderson was thinking they would have to make a halt when he spied smoke drifting from a narrow ravine in the hillside. 'Let's take a look up here,' he shouted, and led the way through thorn scrub until they saw in the gloomy dusk a ramshackle house of bare weather-boards.

'Ahoy, the house,' blacksmith Jed Farris bellowed. 'Anybody in there, come on out with your hands up.'

Anderson indicated to the posse to stay back and went ahead on foot. There were no lights showing in the low-slung joint but smoke was curling from the chimney. He fired off a warning shot from his Creedmore and shouted, 'This is your last chance. Show yourselves or we start shooting.' The house remained sinisterly silent for some moments until a woman's voice called, 'There ain't nobody here. I'm coming out.'

Deputy Cass Clayton had joined the marshal and Anderson gritted out to him, 'Stay well back and keep your head down. They might start shooting.'

The door opened and a tall woman came out. 'They've all gawn,' she said. 'There's only me here.'

'It's Big Kate,' Cass called, going forward to her. 'You're a liar, Kate. Tell Joe and the others to come out. The game's up.'

Anderson heard her swearing by all that was holy that she was the only one in the house. 'You cain't come in,' she screamed. 'No, I ain't lighting a lamp. I'm outa kerosene.'

'Keep back, Cass,' Anderson shouted, but his deputy pushed past her and kicked the door open. As he raised his carbine to aim inside, Kate wrestled his arm up. Buckshot blasted out from inside the door and Cass dropped to the ground as Kate retreated indoors.

At first Anderson thought – hoped – that Clayton might be taking cover, lying doggo. But he had no time to find out for gunfire was now blasting from the shack's windows, bullets ricocheting about his head in a sustained attack. 'Shee-it!' he growled, as he and the posse returned fire, riddling the thin board walls with lead.

There was a pause in the gunfire and the blacksmith roared, 'We've found some hay and we're gonna burn you down, you sons-a-bitches.'

Another fusillade broke out from both sides, one of the posse crying out as he was hit. Silence again. 'We've had enough!' Kate screeched, poking out an arm from the door and waving a pair of white drawers. 'We're coming out.'

When their weapons had been tossed outside Kate appeared, followed by Rosy Joe and John Wesley, their hands raised. 'Don't shoot, fellas,' Wesley begged. 'I didn't kill nobody.'

Anderson darted forward and knelt beside his slumped deputy. He rolled him over. Bloodstains peppered his chest. 'Cass is dead,' he shouted. 'Where's them other bastards got to?'

Kate's protestations that they had gone proved true.

'Santa Cruz sneaked off with the gal,' Rosy Joe told them. 'Ben Watson went with 'em. I didn't realize they weren't here 'til you arrived. They took the cash with 'em. It's all gawn.'

Joe cursed his colleagues in lurid language as Anderson put the cuffs on him. The blacksmith Jed, hammered his fist into his jaw. 'Shut up, you cur,' he shouted, kicking Joe as he fell on the ground. 'Let's string 'em up now, boys. Get it over with. It's all they deserve.'

Anderson jabbed his Remington into the tearful blacksmith. 'That's enough, Jed. We're all upset. But I'm taking 'em back tomorrow. We'll rest here tonight. Truss these three varmints up so they can't move hand or foot, boys. We'll carry Cass inside.'

'What about Lizzie?' Jim Upstone wailed, searching the house for his daughter. 'What are you going to do about her, Marshal?'

'Don't worry, Mr Upstone, I'll catch up with 'em,' Anderson promised. But he wasn't so sure, or, if he did whether Lizzie would be still alive.

As luck would have it the wounded man was Fin Warren. Lead had smashed through his right elbow. It was bad and there wasn't much the marshal could do. 'He was the one man I could rely on,' Anderson gritted out to nobody in particular. 'He won't be doin' no gunfightin' again.'

He scouted out before dawn along the river-bank, but the birds had flown. 'My main priority is to git Fin back to the medic. He's in agony and losing blood. Then I got to get these three buzzards safely under lock and key.'

It was a sombre party who returned, Cass's body slung across his horse. Mrs Clayton started sobbing and screaming. 'I begged Cass not to take this job. I knew this would happen.'

'I tried to warn him,' the marshal muttered, as women gathered around to soothe the deputy's wife and children.

Anderson lodged his prisoners in the pens and took the mare along to the livery to get her shoed. It had grown dark by now and there were a lot of men hanging about giving him menacing looks. Jed Farris doused the red-hot shoe in a bucket of water then nailed it to the grey's hoof. 'There, she's done,' he said and, as he passed behind, he snatched the Remington revolver from the marshal's holster. 'But *we* ain't done yet. I got him, boys.' Several men appeared and grabbed hold of Anderson's arms, tying him back against a post. 'Get the keys off his belt.' The blacksmith produced three stout ropes each looped into a hangman's noose. 'Follow me, men. We got justice to do.'

THE VENGEANCE OF JUDGE LYNCH, screamed the headline as *The Clarion* was rushed out to news stands the next morning. ROSY JOE, BIG KATE AND WESLEY DRAGGED FROM JAIL BY IRATE MOB.

They were marched amid flaming torches along the railroad out of town to a trestle bridge over a declivity. As the nooses were slipped over their heads Wesley begged and grovelled in terror, Kate accepted her fate silently, and Rosy Joe ranted.

'You ought to be down on your knees praying to God to forgive you your heinous sins,' a woman shrieked.

'What's God ever done fer me?' Joe snarled. 'It ain't likely

He's gonna do anythang now. See y'all in Hell.'

'Begone, sinners,' the blacksmith roared, and pushed Rosy Joe, Wesley and Kate off the bridge. Folks craned to see them swing, struggling and choking, until they were finally at peace.

When Jed Farris returned to release the marshal from his bonds he received a straight right to the jaw from Anderson knocking him back over his anvil. 'I oughta arrest you,' he said.

'Lynch law is to be deplored but the people of Abilene mourn a brave deputy, Cass Clayton, our beloved preacher, Revd. Copsey, and two fine citizens, Mayor Hooson and Mr Geppert, now lying dead. None will shed a tear for their vicious murderers or regret the way of their passing.

'Where are you going?' Jane Cox asked that morning when she found Anderson in the stable behind the jail packing his spare mustang with supplies as a pack-horse.

'We're going after 'em,' Anderson grunted out. 'Rosy Joe was so incensed by his pals' treachery he squealed. They're heading south to the Nations. That was their plan. It'll be a long, hard haul.'

Jane glanced at Newt who was tying his blanket roll to the back of the pinto's saddle. 'You're surely not taking the boy? They are dangerous gunmen.'

'I've explained that. He's gotta learn to stand up for himself.'

'I ain't sceered,' Newt piped up. 'I wanna go.'

When the boy ran off to fetch his rifle, Jane pleaded with Anderson. 'Please don't take him. We would be glad to look after him while you're away . . . or if anything happens to you.'

Anderson eyed her and shook his head. 'I was an orphan. Never knew my father. I don't want that to happen to Newt.'

'Are you saying he's your son?'

'Seems so, don't it?' He turned to face her. 'Don't fuss yourself, Jane. We'll be OK. Let's face it, I think you and me are too daggers drawn, too prickly, ever to make bed partners – more's the pity.'

Jane shrugged, helplessly. 'If that's the way you feel . . . but I'll be waiting for you.' She touched his arm. 'Take care, Hank.'

THIRTEEN

To try to make up time, Anderson loaded their horses on to the next Kansas and Pacific train east, through Junction City to Topeka. There he transferred to the Atchison, Topeka and Santa Fe railroad, which rattled south-west to Newton. The town had taken over the mantle of Abilene, its streets packed shoulder to shoulder with roistering Texans, gamblers and fancy women as the last herds rolled in, the saloons open all hours, roulette wheels spinning, even the mayor of the city indulging in the giddy dance with the girls.

'We gotta change here to the new branch line south,' Anderson explained, as he led Newt along to the box car to unload their mounts once more. 'Only opened last September. Goes another fifty miles south to Caldwell on the border of the Nations.'

First stop, though, was Wichita, another thriving cattle town where he decided to stay the night at a cheap hotel. He told Newt to get to bed while he looked around the saloons and bawdy houses asking if anyone had seen their quarry.

'The black stallion, the young dude in black and the purty gal? Yeah, they were here. An older guy with 'em,' the deputy marshal of Wichita, Jim Clarke, told him. 'I noted them because they were high-rollers, showering dollars about like confetti.'

'Yeah, they robbed the bank at Abilene. Didn't you get my wire?'

'I believe we did, Marshal, but by then they had gone,' Clarke shouted above the din. 'You can see we got enough on our hands here without going off on some wild goose chase.'

Maybe that was what it was, Anderson thought, as he tried to get some sleep at the hotel amid the racket of gunshots, wild screams and celebration that went on through the night.

At Caldwell, the end of the track, the marshal there had a similar story. They had been and gone. Big spenders, but they didn't break any laws so he had not concerned himself with them.

'Spend most of my time issuing fines,' he drawled. 'The city pulled in two thousand dollars last month from liquor, gambling licences and prostitution. We got it well-organized.'

'Looks like they've headed south into the Nations,' Anderson announced the next morning as he saddled up. 'It's gonna be like looking for a needle in a haystack from now on.'

Before them stretched a vast area of mountains, rivers and plains where sixty-seven diverse Indian tribes from all parts of the USA had been brought together from their homelands to join the original inhabitants. Most lived in peace, but many were engaged in jealous hostility with each other.

The Nations were also a magnet for white fugitives from justice, bands of lawless men who had grown used to killing in the Civil War and had little incentive to return to their war-torn homes.

'I got no real jurisdiction here,' Anderson said, as they set off. 'But I don't need none.'

'What do you mean?' Newt asked.

Anderson slapped the Remington on his thigh. 'I ain't never been keen on all that legal mumbo jumbo. This is all the jurisdiction I need.'

The first day out they had a stroke of luck, running into an old galoot who was staggering along on foot, leading an overloaded jackass. 'Yeah, I seen 'em,' he hollered. 'The young stud in black was riding two-up, a purty gal hanging on behind him. Her hoss had broke a leg and been shot. They persuaded me to part with my best mule, Mollie.'

'How'd they do that?' Newt asked.

'How'd you think, sonny?' the old guy wheezed. 'With the persuasive power of his six-guns.'

'What you carrying in them sacks?' Anderson asked.

'Salt. Got it from the Great Salt Lake. I'll sell it in Caldwell.' He pointed them on their way. 'That's the way they gawn. You jest keep going, straight as an arrow.'

Sure enough, as they reached the salt plains they saw a line of tracks, two horses and a mule, clearly marked, heading towards the flat horizon. It was a hot, hard trek for twenty miles or so, mirages of water flickering before their eyes in the haze, before they reached the lake, a desolate spot. No sign of human habitation.

Day after day they trudged on, warily and wearily, rationing the water in their canteens. The banks of the Cimarron River made a welcome sight. Newt splashed about as Anderson built a small fire, plucked a partridge he had shot, turned it on a greenwood spit.

'It sure is fun not to have to go to school.'

'This is all the education you need for the moment,' Anderson muttered, as he showed him how to fish for trout. 'Larnin' how to stay alive, that's what counts.'

He let the boy sleep in his soogans, the fire flickering low, keeping watch, his Creedmore between his knees. It was good to lean back in the saddle, rest his bones beneath a canopy of trillions of twinkling stars. Good to get away from the clamour of towns. But there was always the possibility of some renegade redman creeping up on him, cutting his throat, or trying to, to steal his hat, cash, or horses. Or some black-hearted white villain, come to that. After midnight he dozed off, but didn't sleep easy, alert to the slightest unusual sound.

Anderson headed west to hit the North Canadian River, entering a region of harsh crags and ravines, wild broken country. By now he had lost their trail, but he just had a hunch they would head west. Vince Santa Cruz liked the high life too much to hang about in the wilderness for long.

The fine weather of clear blue skies had gone. A

cold wind from the north had set in and, as skeins of geese migrated south, it warned of winter blizzards to come.

'If we follow the river upstream it should bring us back to the plains,' Anderson said one night as they made camp. 'I've a hunch those scallawags aren't far in front. 'He glanced uneasily up at cliffs towering on either side of them. 'Keep your eyes peeled. They could be waiting.'

In the past, Anderson had been wild, not giving a damn about his life, going in, striking first. But he had never had anyone else to worry about. Now, looking at the sleeping boy, he knew he must be cautious. What am I doing? he wondered, pondering whether to give up the chase and go back. What'll happen to him if I'm killed? Nor did the thought of the boy being shot or injured bear contemplation.

Perhaps that was why he became a hard taskmaster to Newt, trying to drum into him the basics of survival in the wilderness. He had to learn to cope by himself. Just in case.

'That ain't the way to make a fire,' he would growl as they made camp beside the swirling river. 'Ain't you larned yet? Make kindling like this. You only need to use one match. There's six there you've wasted. Build the fireplace so it funnels in the wind. That damp green wood's no damn good. Go find some dry stuff.'

He had swiftly cut pine boughs to build a half-bivouac shelter for the night, binding the structure with pliant roots he dug out of the earth, thatching it with needles, spreading some down to make a

147

comfortable bed. 'I guess I got years of experience of living rough. He'll get the hang of it soon enough.'

In the morning they had packed their mounts ready to go when suddenly a bullet whistled past his head, followed by the clap of rifle sound from up on the crags that towered over them. 'Newt!' he screamed. 'Get down!'

Anderson took his own advice, flattening himself in the cover of the rocks as another blue whistler nearly took off his ear, and others rained down, ricocheting, slicing shards of gypsum, as he cowered and looked around desperately for his son.

But Newt, thirty paces away, had had the good sense to do as he was bid and wriggle into cover, too. There was a pause in the fusillade, probably to reload. Anderson took the opportunity to make a dash, keeping low, to grab his Creedmore. He peered over the rocks and aimed a volley of shots from where the puffs of smoke a hundred yards above, had issued.

'Indians!' he hissed, hearing their harsh yelping cries. 'A dozen of 'em. By their shaved heads I'd say Osage.' He squeezed his rifle trigger and one of the heads was smashed like a melon in a spray of blood.

'When I start shooting again get on your horse and get outa here,' he shouted, reloading from his belt. 'Follow the river. Ride for all you're worth.'

'What about you?'

'I'll be OK. I'll follow you.' The boy knelt, biting his lip, ready to go, and when Anderson raised his Creedmore again to keep the Osage war party at bay, he hared away, leaped on his pony and yelled, 'Go,

Rocky! Go!'

Anderson picked his targets, letting Newt get a good start. He spotted a warrior on top of a rock, a warclub in his hand, and potted him, sending him tumbling. There was a cry of wrath as, his sixteen slugs spent, he swung on to the saddle of the grey, caught hold of the pack-mustang's leading rein, and spurred away.

They were lucky. The ravine opened out on to a plain and Newt was already galloping on his way as fast as the cow pony could go. Anderson charged after him, the mare responding to his touch, but hampered by the mustang dragging them back. The marshal glanced back and saw the Osage warriors charging down from the hills, riding bareback, firing their rifles as they rode. Anderson had stuffed the Creedmore in the saddle boot and drew his Remington revolver to return fire.

After half a mile the grey went thudding at full gallop past the boy on his valiant little pinto, mane and tail blowing in the wind. Anderson eased the mare so as not to get too far ahead, but now the Osage, already whooping victoriously, were gradually gaining on them and they knew it.

Suddenly Anderson spotted a military post in the distance, a mile or so away. So near and yet so far. He might have made it on his own. He had roped his gold-plated Winchester to the pack-horse and stuffed his wallet packed with $9,000, his ranch fund, into a flour sack on the mustang for safe-keeping. He was reluctant to do it, but as the grinning warriors' lead whistled past their ears he made the only possible decision. Drawing his scalping knife he cut the pack-mustang free.

It worked. That was what the Osage were interested in. As the pack-horse trailed behind they whooped to go collect their prize, and turned back to inspect it. Anderson and Newt went charging away towards Fort Supply.

As they reached the gate to the stockade the marshal reined in to look and saw the warriors riding away into the wilderness. 'There goes all my immoral earnings and my five hundred dollar rifle,' he muttered, as Newt joined him. He grinned at the boy. 'Quite a chase, huh?'

Argyle was a scattering of clapboard houses and barns, many deserted now, situated on the long panhandle of the Nations known as No Man's Land. Its saloon had long been the hangout of riff-raff, rustlers and outlaws.

Vince Santa Cruz was taunting Lizzie as she sat at a table in the dingy saloon opposite him. 'Show 'em your legs, gal.' He flashed his reckless grin at a bunch of hairy, smelly men in filthy clothes, who were sitting like a bunch of hungry wolves ogling her. 'They ain't seen a purty gal like you around here for an age. Shall I toss you to 'em?'

Lizzie looked none too clean and tidy herself, her blonde hair unwashed and windswept, her dress torn and stained from the weeks of being forced to ride along with Vince and Ben Watson.

Her cheeks were tear-stained as she cast a mournful glance at her tormentor. 'Why are you so horrible to me, Vince? You said you loved me. You said we were going to get wed.'

'That was when you were fresh and virginal as a daisy, Lizzie, 'cause I ain't got a taste for them poxy ol' hoo-ers. But now look at you. You ain't fresh and virginal no more. Any you boys wanna have a poke at her?'

The rough bunch almost slavered at the mouth as they stared at the girl, but they had seen the twin pearl-handled Smith & Wessons on Vince's hips and weren't willing to take her unless he said so. 'Sure,' one slurred, 'if you don't wan' her.'

'Vince, don't do this,' Lizzie pleaded. 'It ain't right.'

The slim young outlaw in his black outfit got to his feet and stepped across. 'I said show 'em your legs,' he said, slapping her viciously across her face, and hauling her to her feet.

'Not my face, Vince,' the girl screamed. 'Not my face.'

'Right!' He grabbed hold of her, sitting down and slinging her across his knees pulled her dress high. 'How's that, boys?'

He began to larrup her with the quirt hanging from his wrist, laughing at her howls. 'That's fer not doin' what I said. Don't that make sense to you, boys?'

He pushed her away and she tumbled to the floor-boards, sobbing and snivelling, trying to cover herself. 'I hate you,' she screamed.

'Ar, sweetheart, you said you loved me.' Vince made

151

a mocking kissing sound. 'Why's you run away with me for?'

'Because I wanted to make the marshal jealous,' she sobbed. 'It's him I love. I hate you. You're evil. You're a killer. You didn't give Mr Hooson a chance.'

'What chance you want me to give that fat fool? He was going for his gun.' Vince pondered her words. 'What's this about the marshal? You mean you an' him . . . before me?'

'No,' she sobbed. 'But I wanted him to.'

Ben Watson had watched the proceedings dourly, his Stetson shading his lined face, hunched in a chair, supping from a bottle of whiskey. 'I'm gittin' tired of your stupid tricks,' he growled. 'I'm gonna take a look outside. There's a storm blowing up.'

Outside it had turned threateningly dark, a gale-force wind banging shutters, blowing tumbleweed down the street. Black clouds were rolling low across the sky, turning the grasslands all about as dark and stormy as a sea. The place was almost a ghost town, two or three folks running into their lairs, trying to batten doors against the gale.

'Hell!' Ben said, as he spied a dark column spiralling across the prairie towards the town. 'That twister's coming this way.'

He was going to go back inside to warn the men, but he paused as he saw two riders fast approaching the town, trying to outrun the pursuing tornado. A man and a boy. 'Where in tarnation they come from?' he growled. 'It's that damn Anderson.'

It was, indeed, the marshal and Newt. As they

hurried their mounts into Argyle, Anderson spotted a storm cellar before a deserted house. 'Here,' he shouted, through the noise of the wind, grabbing hold of its big plank cover and hoisting it up. 'We'll shelter down here.'

Even better was the fact there was a ramp into the deep cellar, and they were able to drag in the frightened mare and pinto. 'You stay here, Newt, whatever you do. I'm gonna take a quick look around. I got time 'fore the twister hits.'

Anderson scrambled out and slammed the cover shut. He lowered his head fighting the hurricane force wind to walk along the street, his hat blown away, his hair splayed across his face. The houses were groaning and creaking, planks and debris flying away, horses at a hitching rail rolling their eyes, trying to pull away in terror.

'Saloon', the scrawled sign announced, but as Anderson started towards it Vince appeared on the sidewalk, standing facing him, hands spread, ready to go for his guns.

A window was smashed behind the marshal and a rifle was poked through. 'How about me?' Watson shouted, his face grimly set.

'Yeah,' Vince yelled. 'Go for it, Marshal. Or don't you like the odds?'

'Hot damn,' Anderson growled, considering his dilemma. The young dude was renowned for striking as fast as a rattler with his pistols. He was by no means sure he could beat him. Even if he did he could expect a bullet in his back. He stood in the howling wind, easing his fingers to go for his Remington. . . .

Suddenly the tornado struck one side of the town, toppling the clapboard houses and false fronts like ninepins. Horses pulled themselves free and galloped away shrieking their terror. Anderson threw himself flat and fired, his six-gun barking out lead. But as the saloon sidewalk trembled Vince had to duck to avoid a flying plank and the shots missed.

As his side of the street was demolished, Ben leaped out of the window to stand amid the dust and debris, tugging his carbine to his shoulder, taking a bead on the marshal. Newt had heaved up the cellar cover to peer out. He rested the Creedmore on the ledge, sighted, and squeezed out a slug. 'Got him!' he shouted, as Ben was hit in the thigh and spun off his feet.

Vince, however, was holding his ground, grinning like a devil from hell, in the turmoil of the twister, both Smith & Wessons in his fists, staring at Anderson, letting him know his time was nigh. Anderson saw Lizzie stagger from the saloon, Vince's rifle held by the barrel. She lunged at the outlaw's elbow making him gasp with pain as he fired, and the shot went wild.

The marshal didn't hesitate. He peered through the semi-darkness and squeezed out three shots, sending Santa Cruz crashing back through the saloon's batwing doors. He rolled over and saw Ben behind him on the ground, grimacing with pain, raising his rifle. Anderson's last bullet hit him in the forehead and Ben Watson slumped dead.

Anderson peered along the street and beckoned to

Newt to get back down, then hauled himself up and ran to jump on to the sidewalk, catching hold of Lizzie, who appeared about to faint. He hauled her inside the saloon and saw a bunch of ragged, frightened men flat on their faces waiting for the twister to pass.

Among them was Santa Cruz, lying on his back, his left-hand revolver held up and pointed their way. Blood spurted from his mouth and the Smith & Wesson fell to the floor. Vince forced a grin and gasped, 'You win. Good ol' Lizzie – never trust a damn woman.'

As soon as it had hit, the twister had passed, demolishing one side of the town in its wake. The men on the saloon floor clomped off to run after their frightened horses. Anderson went and pulled back the storm flap. 'You OK, son? That was a fine shot. You sure saved my bacon.'

They found Vince's stallion angrily whinnying and kicking inside the wrecked stable behind the saloon.

Lizzie whispered, 'I've something to show you.' She went over to a corn bin where the two robbers had stashed the stolen cash. 'They spent quite a bit but there's still about eighteen thousand dollars there.'

'Whoo!' Anderson gave a whistle of awe as he pulled the wads of greenbacks from the flour sacks and counted them out on top of the corn bin. 'Eighteen thousand three hundred and forty smackeroos. A man could buy a damn fine ranch with this, an' stock, too, out in California. We could live in clover.'

'Let's do it, Hank.' Lizzie's eyes shone bright blue with excitement as she hugged hold of him. 'Let's go West and git wed. All of us could be rich an' happy together for ever.'

'For ever's a long time, Lizzie.' Anderson nudged her aside. 'But it sure is a tempting idea. We could ride north through the Black Mesa mountains up to Pueblo and Cheyenne, catch the Central Pacific to Frisco.'

'Do it, Hank,' Lizzie huskily urged. 'We can change our names. Nobody would know.'

'Yeah, I guess that gold-plated rifle with my name on will turn up one day. Folks will think the Injins got me.' Anderson packed the bank notes back in the two sacks, tied them together and slung them over the stallion's neck. 'In fact, it's a perfect idea.'

He led them outside. 'You can ride my mare, Lizzie.'

The girl stood there, tenderly touching her backside through her torn dress. 'Gosh, that's gonna be painful. Vince was horrible to me. He was gonna make me go with those men. He beat me bad.'

'Give you a whupping, did he?' Anderson gave her his lean-jawed grin, caught hold of her and hoisted her on to the mare's saddle. 'You'll be OK. We'll take it easy.'

Lizzie stroked her blonde hair from across her tear-stained face. 'I must look a sight.'

'You look fine.'

'Can you forgive me, Hank? For going away with him?'

156

'Ain't nuthin' to forgive.' The saloon-keeper was dragging Vince out on to the sidewalk by his bootheels. 'He don't look so cocksure now, does he? Be warned, Newt, that's what happens to handsome young dogs like him who figure they're fancy-shootists. They end up dead.'

He bent over Vince's black-clothed corpse and closed his eyes. 'Still, these will be more use to us now than to him.' He unbuckled the gun belt and held the pearl-handled Smith & Wessons aloft. 'I'll teach you how to use these, Newt, when you're older, as long as you promise me you'll only use 'em in self-defence.'

'Gee, Pa,' Newt cried. 'I sure will. I promised Ma.'

Anderson stuffed the pistols in the stallion's saddle-bags and swung aboard. 'Right. You ready to go, boy?'

'You mean to California, Pa?' Newt jumped on to his pinto. 'You mean we're gonna steal all that money? Would that be right?'

'What money?' the saloon-keep asked. 'Who are you, mister?'

'I ain't nobody.' Anderson sent the stallion prancing and clipping around in a high-stepping figure of eight to get the feel of him. 'Maybe I'll put this fine-spirited fellow to my mare. It'll be the start of our own stud.' He hauled in and tossed a silver dollar to the 'keep. 'Bury them two for me, will ya?'

Anderson spurred the stallion shooting forwards to the edge of town, but paused, staring towards the north-west as the other two caught up. 'You don't think it would be right, do ya, boy? Heck, what did them greedy bankers ever do for the South?' He met

Newt's eyes. 'On the other hand I guess we'd allus be lookin' over our shoulder wonderin' if a lawman or Pinkerton detective was gonna catch up.'

'Don't take no notice of Newt,' Lizzie pleaded. 'He's just a kid. He don't know his own mind.'

'Nope, it's you don't know your own mind, Lizzie, like I told you that time. You got some growing up to do.'

'You're not gonna give all that back?' the girl screeched. 'Surely?'

'Jeez!' Anderson sighed. 'Goin' straight ain't easy. An' you ain't making it any easier, gal.' He leaned across and squeezed her hand. 'I'm sorry. It ain't you I love. It wouldn't be no good. I gotta take you back.'

He turned the stallion and set off at a lope across the prairie, heading due north-east towards Abilene.

'Wait for us, Pa,' Newt whooped. 'We ain't all riding high-powered steeds.'

Jane Cox was standing on the sidewalk outside the newspaper office one morning several days later when she saw them ride in. Her heart seemed to jump into her mouth as she saw Anderson stop outside the saddler's store and hand the dusty, ragged girl down, escort her inside.

Newt spotted Jane and rode his pinto fast across. 'Pa's come back 'cause he wants to be with you, Jane. We caught up with them. We've got the stolen cash.'

The marshal came from the store and started on foot up the wide dusty street towards them. 'Thank you, Newt,' Jane whispered, and set off at a run, blinking tears from her eyes, uncaring what folks thought. Anderson caught her warm body and held her tight as Jane kissed his lips and whispered, 'Thank God you're safe.'

'Hey,' he said, gently wiping tears from her cheeks. 'You didn't think I'd leave you, did ya? That's somethang I ain't never gonna do.'

AUTHOR'S NOTE

Although the main characters and events in this story are fictional, they are based on people mentioned in court proceedings, eye-witness descriptions and stories from various newspapers published in the 1870s in the Kansan cowtowns.